The Skinback Fusiliers

Unknown Soldier

ISBN: 978-1-4476-5966-2

Contents

Here Comes the Bullet

Three Ways to Leave the Army

Introduction

The first thing I need to say about this book is that it was not written as an attack on British soldiers. My family has a long tradition of providing fighting men (and women who joined but did not fight as such). One of my uncles was a decorated hero during World War II, several others fought, and my father always resented the fact that as an engineer he was not allowed to go.

Two of my cousins, long after that huge war, joined up and served for many years, also seeing active service. Incidentally, they also taught me most of the filthy songs I know, including the one that provided the title of the book. It was later taken up by Arsenal fans, which we all found very strange.

The question as to why young men join nowadays is not as simple as it might seem. I wrote this book through long friendships and conversation with young people, many of whom had hankered after a military career for years for reasons best described as idealistic. They saw it as a noble thing to do; the chance to fight, and even die, for their country and their birthright. One should be very cautious before one mocks. Look at Wootton Bassett.

It is also true, however, that for the mass of Britain's soldiers, the reasons are heartlessly mundane. The three I got closest to, the bearers of this story, joined because they felt they had no real alternative, and because they had been lied to, which they learned over a period of a few short months.

Andy had blown his chance of proper schooling skyhigh, and thought the army would give him a civvie street career. Ashton, a young black man skating around the fringes of criminality, joined to escape that yawning chasm. Shahid had inchoate fears based in his religion and community; he wanted to explore the idea of brotherhood. They were all sure, at first, that they had done the right thing. And they were all insistent, when they left, that for other men it was no problem, no big deal.

In that, sadly, they are almost certainly wrong. The stats for crime and homelessness, drunkenness and marital breakdown among ex-servicemen are truly horrendous. The government, inevitably, lies and fudges endlessly – because it has to. At the very least, if the truth were known, their supply of cannon fodder might dry up. As ex-soldier Ross Williams put it after serving time for being absent without leave from the Iraq war "The army uses up and spits out young working class men in pursuit of their bloody, illegal wars." Williams, incidentally, shared a cell at Colchester with Lance Corporal Joe Glenton, who now addresses anti-war meetings, and who said of this book: "Reading it was like being back in the mob."

The more I talked to my friends and contacts, the more my own anger grew. I wanted to present what I saw as the realities to people who would not normally have access, or indeed much interest, in them. I also wanted to get under the skin of people who would not normally even read a book, people who might think joining the army is a reasonable way out of poverty, or is generally "a good thing." It's not. It's not even a necessary evil, if one believes the magnificent Simon Jenkins. He argued in June 2010 that the whole of the armed forces should be scrapped because "We are safer than at any time since the Norman conquest. Yet £45bn is spent defending Britain against fantasy enemies."

Because I wanted this book read, then, I wrote it in the terms and language of the people I knew and liked and admired in the military. Whether they all believe me or not, I want to show them that they are the victims of a vile and cynical deal, which serves nobody's interests but the government's. Our soldiers are paid, pro-rata, far less than the minimum wage – you don't go home for your tea at the end of a shift if you happen to be in Helmand and your wife and children live in Catterick – and if they do get shipped back injured they have to compete for civilian hospital places. Any special treatment ends as soon as they reach minimum standards of recovery. Mental health problems are disregarded and robustly lied about, which is one reason why so many ex servicemen live on the streets, and partner and child abuse is terrifyingly high. They risk everything for their masters, and receive a vanishing minimum in return. After ten years of prevaricating the government still sends them out in snatch Land Rovers to be killed by IEDs, and now actually boasts that replacements will be available – by the end of 2011. It's hard to believe that they aren't completely mad.

I call this book a novel because I can't think of any other designation, and because I am a much-published novelist, as well as being a playwright and TV and radio script writer. I tried hard to get it published through the normal channels, but it was not the sort of thing publishers seem to want. I was even sacked by my agent, after more than twenty years. But every thing and every person in it, every attitude and every conversation, is grounded solidly in truth, sourced from hundreds of hours of conversations, and piles of notes and letters and scraps of paper. None of the boys is dead, none of them is still in the army. My hope for this book would be that it could help persuade some others to achieve the same result. Does that sound unpatriotic?

Twelve Good Men and True

One

I know the meaning of a really bone night out, and it hit me there was a good one coming up when our corporal suggested we went out on the town to kick-start a few Pakis. It wouldn't have been that unusual, I suppose, except it was about an hour after we'd had a mega bullshit talk on race relations. The major finished off with "be nice to Johnny Wog, it's what the British Army do, it's called building trust," and it made me wonder if I'd made the right career choice. Better off as a shithouse cleaner, say. Better paid, in any case!

The weird thing was, he wasn't a Colonel Blimp-style crusty, although he did tend to talk like something off the films. He was quite young, and seemed quite friendly in a stuck up kind of way, but he was completely out of touch. I mean, for fuck's sake, Johnny Wog. Embarrassing. What school do these wankers go to?

The Lance Jack's name was Martin, talking of race relations, and he was a Scouser, which meant he was a fully paid up hater anyway. He hated blacks (nignogs) and Asians (Pakis), and worst of all he hated cops – it came with the territory. In fact he hated everybody, really, except for other Scousers, it was like something in their mother's milk, and if there hadn't been any Asians in this one-horse town, he'd have chosen someone else to give a kicking to. But there were Asians, and they were Banglas, which meant the Asians in our crew could join in the battering as well, which was handy.

The thing was, it was like at school. White kids beat up the Pakis, that was normal. Then the Paks beat up the Bangladeshis, and we all joined in to give the gippoes shit. In some schools black kids were in the mix, but we only had two in my dump, and they were ginormous. Even the teachers didn't shit on them.

When I say the Asians in our crew I mean just one, in actual fact, and I glanced across to see how he'd reacted to the corporal's crack. His name was Shahid, and by one of those things you can never understand, he'd got to be my sort of mate. He was sort of lanky, sort of soft-skinned, and he had these big brown eyes that could have caused him lots of aggro in the army if he hadn't been so hard. In the navy he'd have been rammed to death, if you get my drift. But he had this way of smiling at people he despised that really put them on the spot – because they didn't know if he was being submissive or tekkin piss, and he had that look on now. Just to confirm it, like, he winked, on the side the corporal couldn't see.

"Well, you've got a problem there," he said, with his funny little crooked smile. "There ain't no Pakis in this town to kick. Tek it from me."

"Fuck off," said Martin. His eyes were small and glittery, because he guessed he was being set up. "What you on about, you fairy? Place is fucking crawling with 'em. Fucking vermin."

"Ah," said Shahid. "There you might be right. But I promise they're not from Pakistan. They're Bangla men. A very different kettle." He gave a little tiny pause. Timed to a millisecond. "That's the problem, innit? We all look the same to a Scouser."

There were ten or twelve of us in the room, and we took the chance to have a little laugh at that. Martin didn't mind because he'd got his dig in first – he'd called Shahid a fairy – and he hadn't kicked up about the basic proposition, which was to go out looking for a bit of white supremacy, when it boiled down to it. It would be a pretty craphole Friday evening if we didn't have a fight – black, white or khaki – specially 'cause the billet they'd tipped us into was the pits. The so-called Naafi bar had one pool table and no Sky, and the lager you could tell was piss just by looking at it. In any case it was full of Paras, and you don't mix with them, do you? If you want your face.

"Banglas, is it?" Martin answered in the end. Dazzling Scouser wit coming up, you could tell it from a mile off. "I don't care if they're the wild men of Borneo. They live in this dump, so they deserve a kicking. Who's in? Everybody? Gough?"

We looked at Goughie then like a band of monkeys, like Mart had knew we would. Psychology he'd've called it if he could pronounce the word, but it wasn't rocket science, trust me. Every unit's got a Gough, and everybody looks at him, because to look at him is to give yourself a boost. Feeling down? Look at Goughie. Feeling clumsy, dozy, lost? There's your man. Wondering if you've reached the bottom of the slide, if there's nowhere further down to go? Well, you get my meaning.

He didn't have a first name, Johnnie Gough. Whoops – giveaway. He'd been older than most of the recruits when we started, maybe nineteen, maybe even twenty, and he was born to fail, it was writ all over him in letters ten foot high. He was tall, and pale, and spotty, and after the first few weeks he never spoke, unless a corporal or a sergeant made him, just to have a laugh. The best bet was he'd be a suicide, a Deepcut Diver. I shared with him up at camp in training. He used to cry himself to sleep.

"Eh, Gough? Eh? Are you fucking deaf, or something? I said are you fucking deaf? Geddit?!"

Goughie nodded.

"Yes, Mart."

"Yes Mart what?"

Gough blinked at him. The corporal sneered.

"What, Mart?"

"What Mart, yes Mart, what? Kick a Paki is what. Is that what you want to do, eh? Is it?"

Gough blinked again. His spots stood out against the skin. There were small cuts on his face, from shaving.

"Yes, Mart."

Mart crowed triumphantly.

"So you'll be on a charge then, won't you, you racist twat? It's against the law to kick a Paki till we get to fucking Helmand!"

Shahid put in quietly: "He's in the clear then, ain't he? He'll be kicking Banglas. You're all right, Goughie. Panic over."

"Soft get," the corporal told Shahid, but not with any poison in his voice. "You'll get a reputation you will, Stanley, standing up for wankers. Goughie got you on a promise, has he?"

Shahid just grinned, ignoring him (and the joke: Paki-Stan, geddit?) and everyone started sorting out their gear. We were on a course down in this barracks, half uniform, half coveralls, so it was a case of out of work clothes, shower, dress up in finery, stuff some scran down our necks, and wander. The fact we wouldn't be in uniform meant nothing in a town like this – they were trained to instant recognition. If there was any slappers looking for a bit of beef-bayonet, there we were, and the local lads would keep well clear because we were mob-handed. The normal plan was get tanked, get laid, and find someone to batter who wasn't in the Paras.

It all went pretty well, up to a point. It was a right old dump to start with, and you had to work dead hard to get a buzz. It was way out in the country, see, but not the real country, like we were used to, hills and rocks and stuff like that, it was all green and rolling with piss-wet trees and woody stuff, on the edge of the training ranges. The barracks was just out of town, on a quiet leafy road, and it was raining, but we didn't mind the walk, we didn't have to. Back in Catterick it would have been taxis, or some lads who had cars, but here the taxis wouldn't pick up squaddies, on account of too much vomit, we'd been told, too much fucking off without paying. It was a pisstake really, I reckon: we had no trouble getting taxis other times. But it suited the landlord of the nearest pub, didn't it? I mean, anyone who's got a licence and a garden shed in falling distance of a barracks has died and gone to heaven. Simples.

I was first up to the bar for my shout – me and Shahid – which was a trick I'd been trained up to by my sister, who's done bar work since she was knee high to a turd. The landlord was a fat aggressive sort of bloke, and he didn't bother with a smile.

"Two pints of lager, please, mate."

"We don't do lager."

I was gobsmacked.

"You what?"

"No call for it."

"Come on, Tiny! Get your finger out!" That was the corporal. Pissed off I'd got served first. Stirring it.

"What d'you mean no call for it? There's twelve of us here, we're calling for..."

A smile began to form.

"You can always bugger off," he said. "It's only two miles to the next good pub." Two lies in two seconds: not bad, eh? But while I was wondering how far to push it, Martie Martin took his chance. He elbowed me to one side, grinning at the landlord.

"Four whiskies, mate, and make 'em big'uns, eh? For the grown-ups in this sorry fucking lot."

I got in second, though, that was something. Scotch for me and gin for Shahid, with a tonic ("Fucking hell, Stan – you really are a poof," said Mart), so the rest decided they'd go exotic too. It was Pernod, Drambuie, Pernod AND Drambuie, rum and ginger wine, you name it, and the landlord raked the cash in with a happy Christian feeling in his heart. No smile, though, although his prices were sky high.

If we'd had brains, if we'd had any common sense at all, we'd just have had the one, then gone on and found a proper place to have some fun in, wouldn't we? But we didn't. It was just one more, and just one more, and then one for the road. If we'd had brains we wouldn't have been there in the first place. If we'd had brains we wouldn't have been in the army, would we?

Next stop the 'Stan, know what I mean, the fucking Sandpit? Next stop mopping up the shit the Yankies've laid out for us, the burned up babies, the blown up brides and grooms, the bits of hearts and minds they scatter round the place. They kicked us out of Sangin because our government starved us of the gear to do the job with, and next stop is catch the bullet. Corporal fucking Martie's Volunteers. The Skinback Fusiliers...

Two

Next stop, in fact, turned out to be a lot of drink, a few taxi rides I don't really remember, Martie Martin getting completely arseholed and pulling rank like there wan't no tomorrow, and a little bit of sweet revenge. It cost a tooth or two, a drop of blood, a fair few swollen lips, but it was worth it. It was down to Shahid, too. It was Shahid's big night out.

It was the taxis started it. When Mart had had enough Grouse down his neck he got fed up of the Pub with No Beer, and tried to shift us out. He couldn't get a cab for love or money, and the landlord wasn't going to help clear out his only customers, was he? Then Shahid disappeared into the rain to use his mobile, and turned up two shagged out old Nissans, three times round the clock, with two shagged out old Bangla drivers who took all twelve of us, because the price was right. I could see the tarmac through the hole underneath my trainers, which was a good thing really. It let in enough air to blow the exhaust fumes and the farts away.

"Christ, what a shitheap, couldn't you do no better than this?" said Martie, with Scouser gratitude. "Ask him where the best place is. Booze and tarts, that's all we want. It's not a lot to ask, is it, you useless Paki twat?"

The driver, a harmless sort of geriatric without a lot of teeth, glanced back with a big smile on his face.

"Sorry, sir, I am a Muslim. I do not drink."

He and Shahid laughed out loud, then talked quietly and rapidly between themselves. Urdu or something, maybe, like the kids back at our school. Then Sha winked at the lance corporal.

"The Southern Cross," he said. "All tastes catered for. Best fucks, best fights, best fixes. And he'll tell me where we can go on to after, if you really want some trouble. The Bangla boot boys, where no white man dares to tread!"

"Just fucking try me," said Corporal Martin. You could see his chest and shoulders swelling. And his head. "Just let 'em fucking wait and see... Ask him! Go on! Ask him!"

"I will," said Shahid. "It'll be a pleasure. He'll want a big tip, though. He'll be letting his own side down, won't he? That must be worth a few."

"How much spare you got?" said Martie, punching Goughie in the ribs. "Come on, you tight cunt, it's a fair point, ain't it, la'! You'll be my fucking friend for life."

It's easy in the army if you know the rules. Poor Goughie did. He'd learned the hard way.

As shit pubs in shit towns go, the Southern Cross was pretty normal for a shit night out, and at least the landlord knew what lager was. We did drinking, smoking, chatting up the local talent, dancing, shouting till your bloody voice went hoarse, you name it. Some of the totty looked half-willing in a dozy, empty Friday night sort of way, but I wasn't in the mood to try it on. My mum – who shouldn't know, as far as I can see – told me when I joined up that the uniform would have them flocking to me, and God knows why, it seems to work an' all. She told me to be careful, and she blushed dead scarlet, and I thought of her one night when I was having some tart up against a wheelie bin, and it ran away from us. I thought of my mother and my sister, and I picked myself up and buggered off and left her lying there. She shouted something that I didn't want to hear, and I got put on a charge next morning because I'd tore me keks. Yeah, mum was right. I should've been more careful, shouldn't I?

By the time Martie told us we were moving out, everyone had had enough and didn't bother arguing. Our resident druggies, Josh Peters, Chas Hicks and Geordie George had scored thanks to Wasambu (Sambo – he was Ugandan) who homed in on anything illegal, didn't use it, but always took a cut, while the booze fanatics Timmo Hawes and Big Dave Hughes had got their skinful along of Mart. Ashton, who was as black as Sambo but English and a total gash hound, led the charge towards the tarts, followed by Pete Bollocks Bowyer (more bollocks than brains), and Billy Simmonds, known as Billy 'Unt because he was one. Ashton was my mate, along with Shahid, and denied he was a gash hound through thick and thin, because he was engaged to girl in Manchester who'd cut his balls off if she knew. To prove his purity, he'd settled for just a blow job round the back.

It was Martie Martin – hard as arseholes as he liked to see himself – who had come off worst, he was as pissed as a pudden on a legless high. He'd bummed two twenties off of Geordie George and made it clear he wouldn't get it back, and he'd told Josh Peters that he'd fucked his sister, which for all I know was true, she was known to put out for a wrap when desperate. He'd told anyone who'd listen that Sambo was a Zulu prince, and had gone from Stan to Shag to Shithead Paki Ponce with Shahid, and demanded that he found that club the taxi man had promised us. So Shahid did. And it served Mart fucking right. We had a well good laugh.

It was a set-up, obviously, even the dimmest buggers in our team knew that except the corporal, which says it all, I guess. It was a dead hole with a little Asian bouncer on the door, who wasn't big enough in fact to bounce a ball, and it was laid out for a bit of drinking and not much else at all. There were a few blokes sitting about in corners, drab as drab, and tell the honest truth it could have been a rest room behind a taxi firm. Maybe that's what it was. Maybe they were mini-cabsters on a break. Some of them were even drinking tea.

I looked at Shahid's face to get a hint at least, but I got absolutely nothing. He had his easy smile on, and he was making big friendly gestures with his arms, as if to say "well here it is, lads, enjoy!" It clicked quite quickly, though, that he'd brought us here to have a laugh was all, to show the lance up for a wanker, to take the monumental piss. With this magic get-out clause for him – it was all the taxi driver's fault, the lousy Bangla toerag. Quite honestly I didn't mind at all, I thought that it was pretty smart. Except that there'd be trouble over it, when Mart got Shahid back to camp. I thought he'd have his bloody guts for garters.

19

For a moment it was like something from the films the OC showed us in the training for Afghanistan. The Asians looked at us, we looked at the Asians, and it was like East meets West, the merging of the minds and cultures, the road to better understanding – not. They were sitting down, with beards and puzzled faces, and we were standing over them, tall, and drunk, and arrogant. The master race.

"This place stinks," said Big Dave Hughes. "I need a pissing drink."

"But where's the tarts?" said Peter Bollocks Bowyer. "You said we'd get some tasty Moslem minge."

"Hey! Mohammed!" said Corporal Martin to a seated man, an old man with white hair and beard. "We paid good cash for this, Grandpa! We want crumpet."

There are some things that you just don't say, I reckon, in a certain situation, and in three seconds we'd said three of them, with knobs on. So "Run," yelled Shahid, and as half of us shot towards the front door, a dozen lads with sticks burst through another way to batter us. Our boys barged through them to follow us – Chas Hicks knocked the bouncer over like a ninepin – which left Martie, Bollocks and Big Dave to do their version of Custard's Last Stand. Outside we stood and listened for five minutes to let them make their mark on history – because no one liked them anyway – and then we did our duty and waded back in, freshened and regrouped.

It was very dark now – lights had been turned off – and Shahid did a lot of Urdu shouting while we all got punched and kicked and punched and kicked them back, but it didn't last that long. Fights look good on films or telly, but they don't do much harm unless

someone draws a blade. The Asian lads had won in their terms –
they'd driven out the invaders, hadn't they? – so they didn't bother
to come outside and risk the coppers bringing white man's justice in.
That can be expensive, if you're not a white.

We didn't get a taxi, though – funny that, but no one seemed to
want to know us – and it was a long walk in the lashing rain. Lance
Corporal Martin had a broken nose – which was nice – and there
were some cuts and loosened teeth or so, but all in all it had been
a good successful Friday night. When we got back to the camp,
Martie lost his sense of balance and fell down and smashed his face
on the lavvy pan, then threw up all down himself. No one really
tried to help him, much.

"Mission accomplished," said Shahid, as we rolled into our pits.
"And as usual, God were on our side. Amazing how that works, ent
it?"

Three

We had a lie-in in the morning, which we well needed, given it had been our first night out since we'd been posted to this hell hole. In fact they'd been working us like ten-pee tarts, with no time off for good behaviour, to show us who was boss. We were actually down here to be the "enemy," to be the targets in some hard-man training for the Paras. Not as punch bags, no way, they would have murdered us, they had an image to keep up. But every day we had to go out on the ranges, and make like "aggressors" or "insurgents" to be tracked down and "eliminated," ie killed. It was good hard dirty filthy graft.

I thought I was the first to wake up in my room, it was so quiet, but when I opened my eyes, thinking of Bridget, I saw another pair, big brown ones, staring at me. They were pretty close, because this camp was built before the dawn of time, and in them days there were eight beds in it, not four like now. In them days, Shahid's nose would have been down my bleeding throat. He grinned at me.

"Sleeping Beauty," he said. "Shall we go breakfast, or just stay in bed and enjoy the reek of dried-up blood and vomit?"

"Fuck off," came a muffled voice from opposite. "Just fuck off and shut your fucking row up."

It was the corporal. He'd not died in the night, then. Ah well. I blinked my eyes a few times, testing. Not even a headache. Brilliant.

"What time is it?"

"Fuck off! Fuck off the fucking noise, you fucking arseholes!"

"Gone eight o'clock. We'll get talked about. We'll miss— Fucksake, Martie! What have you done to your fucking face?"

Corporal Martin had suddenly sat up. Jesus, what a fright. The one eye you could see was wild. Especially when he realised where he was.

"Christ," he said. "Whose bed is this? Christ fucking Jesus!"

"It's okay, Mart," said Shahid, soothingly, "it's Billy's bed, but Billy didn't stay. You're still a virgin."

"Christ," said Corporal Martin. He was really shocked.

"I'm not kidding you," Shahid said. "You were drunk enough to lose your honour, but you still said no. Are you a Catholic, by any chance?"

The last head poked out of the covers, bleary eyed. It was Big Dave Hughes. He'd been pissed as well, completely wrecked. Still big enough to tip Martie into Billy's pit, though.

"You watch your fucking lip," said Mart aggressively to Shahid. "I'll put you on a fucking charge."

Shahid winked at me.

"Pals' night out," he said. "All equals now, Lance. Don't you re-member that bit?"

He suddenly flung his covers back and stood up, tall and willowy. He had on a tee-shirt and boxers. He reached out for his shells.

"I won't interfere with your ablutions, ladies," he said. "Me and Tiny are off to get some breakfast, right Tiny? We'll make sure the butler keeps your coffee warm."

I shifted fast now. Fair enough to rip the piss off Martin, but if Big Dave had heard the "ladies" bit we could end up dead. If he un-derstood it, that is. Hard to tell with Dave, though. He had reverse reactions. His reflexes worked the wrong way round. Sometimes he twitched his leg because the MO had tapped his kneebone three weeks before. I grabbed me gear and scarpered.

The breakfast, as predictable, was total crap. Not so long ago, my Mum had told me, the government decided squaddies ought to get more proper stuff to eat, you know, Jamie Oliver-type sort of bollocks about how actual food would make us better fighters, all change for fresh veg and pork from proper pigs. Yeah, and the Pope's a Jew.

"What's up with you, then?" Shahid said, as I looked at the stuff on the electric hotplates. He dished out half a ton at random. "It's only bleeding food, you div."

Have you ever seen fifty fried eggs floating in warm oil where they've been for half an hour? Have you ever seen bacon twisted into lengths of black and yellow corpse intestines? Fancy it, do you? Join the British Army. You can have fried bread, too. Handy for dabbing on your piles.

"Them baked beans look like last night's sick," I said. "All pink and lumpy." I took some bits of toast, and some marge and jam, and followed him towards a table. "Anyway, ain't this lot against your religion, you bloody heathen? You're not allowed it, are you?"

"Nah," he said, "that's pig and stuff, but this is champion for Muslims. I don't know *what* it is, granted – but pork it ain't, I guarantee it. Next you'll be telling me you believe in God."

I couldn't really make Shahid out, quite honestly, so I picked up a bit of toast and crunched it, and watched him fill his hole with shite. He dabbed his lips with a slice of soggy bread as if it was a serviette.

"Or maybe it's your escape plan," he went on. "Starve yourself to death and get out that way, is it? I know you've got a death-wish, Paki-lover."

I gaped.

"Fuck off," I said. "I think the food is shite, that's all. And I ain't a fucking Paki-lover. I've *known you too fucking long*."

"Yeah, maybe that's why they call you it," he said, not laughing at the joke. "Hanging about with me and so on. You didn't even notice how they looked at you when we came in just now, did you?"

Well, that was truth and no mistake, I hadn't noticed anything. I find messtimes the worst part of the lot, best done switched off, if you follow me. The stink, the stainless steel, the dirty fork prongs, the food, the grease, I try to stick me mind in neutral. But I still didn't get what he was driving at.

"I wouldn't call 'em Pakis, anyway," I said. "It's illegal, innit? Racial insults. Did you miss the lectures, or don't you care?"

"I don't have to care," he said. "I've got immunity. I can call a spade a spade, you ask Ashton! But you don't do it anyway, do you? Why not? Are you scared you'll go to prison?"

"Very funny," I said. "Hey – what d'you call a Paki with a crossbow?"

Shahid smiled.

"William Patel! D'you get it? See? I called you Paki!"

"And you're a racist git," he said. "What d'you call a sarcastic cowboy?"

"I dunno. Go on."

"Tex Piss!"

We were being looked at now, I noticed that, and no mistake. Not only sitting with a Paki, but laughing with him, too. And then in walks Corporal Martin, with Big Dave Hughes and Billy 'Unt. His face was terrible, and he got a storm of yells and wolf whistles. He gave a little bow all round.

"You should see the others, though!" he said, to all and sundry. "Two still in hospital is what I heard. Billy – get's a cup of tea. Sausage, beans and eggs, okay, four sugars. And hash browns if they've got 'em."

"Come on," said Shahid. "My bullshitometer's going to blow a fuse. D'you want a smoke? I've got a bit of weed."

The corporal tried to stop us. As Shahid stood up, he beamed in on him like a (one-eyed) laser gun. His body was bunched up for trouble. He pulled Big Dave towards him by the arm.

"Ah," he said. "The target. D'you want to score some points, Davie my friend?"

Dim Dave looked stupid as per usual, but me and Shahid got the message fast enough. I got up too, quick but casual. Trouble was, he was between us and the door.

"Oi, Paki" he said. "Where d'you think you're going? You owe me, bastard. And you, wanker."

The interest-level shot up like a rocket. The chat-level went down to balance it. We had an audience.

Shahid stared into Martin's face as he walked up to him. If he was nervous it didn't show at all. I kept my end up best way that I could. A thumping was unlikely here, even with a moron like Big Dave as strong-arm man. But if a lancejack takes against you, things can get quite rough. There's a lot of shit a lance can put your way. Shed loads. And shit always rolls downhill.

Billy dodged back to reinforce the human wall, but me and Sha were fast, and for the moment they moved back, hemmed in by plastic chairs and tables. A low whoop went up – appreciation of the tactics.

"Come on, Paki!" came a sudden yell – anonymous. "Knock his other fucking eye out!"

That wasn't going to help, and Shahid tried to defuse it.

"What's going off?" he said. "There's plenty breakfast left. Billy – get the man that cup of tea, why don't you?"

Martin was four-square now, dead in front of him, his chin stuck out like a cartoon ape.

"You fucking set me up, you little bastard," he began. "You and them Paki poofters in that shithole."

"Bloody hell," said Shahid. "Banglas, I told you, not——"

"Shut it! You're fucking dead, you are! You're going to——"

Just at that moment the double doors swung open, and Corporal Martin shut his mouth so fast he almost bit his tongue off. He'd been shouting, and the whole damn world could hear, inside and out the room. It was an officer, one I didn't know, one of their lot, not ours. He was a big man, a captain. Silence reigns and we all get wet. You could've heard a pin drop.

"Lance Corporal Martin, isn't it?" he said. His voice was calm and pleasant. That stuck-up tone they all have, even the ones who think they're normal blokes like you or me. The sort of tone that makes you want to smash their faces in. The voice of reason, I don't think.

"Yessir! Sorry, sir!"

"Sorry for what?" said the captain. His eyes took in Martin's mashed up mug. I caught a gleam of "target" in his own eye. They could come down big on that sort of thing, when it suited them. I saw him glance at Shahid. Bruised mouth, slight cut to the eyebrow, he'd not got out entirely unscathed himself.

"Well?" the captain said. "Have you two men been fighting? Is that what you're sorry for? Look at your face, man!"

Tough order that, looking at your own face, but no one thought to laugh. He could smell blood, it was standing out a mile. Bad enough to hit a squaddie – bullying! It just doesn't happen in the Army does it, it's a well-known fact! But to hit an Asian – sweet! If Shahid played his cards right, old Martie's days with a stripe were severely numbered. He wouldn't even touch the sides, they'd throw him down the road – and it was no skin off this captain's nose, it wouldn't be his outfit going short, would it, just brownie points and no mistake. Zero tolerance! No racists here! He'd probably get the frigging MBE.

Martie was sweating on it. He wasn't so thick he couldn't see it coming. Big Dave Hughes just looked confused.

"No, sir!" said Corporal Martin. "We ain't been fighting, sir! I walked into a door!"

"A door with fists? We don't have doors with fists down here, Lance Corporal. They're civilised down here. The doors."

"Door with a door knob, sir." He stopped. "Honest truth, sir, I were pissed. Friday night, sir." Another pause. He swallowed. "Honest truth, sir, we got in a fight. In town. Not just me, sir, few of us. All mates." Last pause. Covering all the options. "Then I walked into a door."

"They jumped us, sir," said Billy 'Unt. "In a club, sir. Some P—"

Even Billy saw which way that line was going. He stopped. His mouth hung open.

"Some pricks," said Shahid, looking at the captain's eyes. "Sorry about his language, sir. Billy... well, he's from Rochdale, sir. We got jumped by some yobboes. Scallies. They were after squaddies, sir, and any bunch would do. We copped for it."

"Well, I hope you came off best!" the captain said. It came out automatic-like, he couldn't help himself.

"Yessir!" said the corporal, just as automatically. A sort of grateful grin, half proud, half rueful. It brought the captain to his senses, maybe. Too much stupid role-play. His face went severe again.

"You're a non-commissioned officer, not a thug," he said. "On your honour, is this true? Were you set upon by local yobs? No provocation?"

"Yes, sir!" said Corporal Martin. "No, sir! No provocation, sir!"

"I'm a Muslim, sir," said Shahid. "We don't tell lies, sir, we're not allowed to, Allah says. Lance Corporal Martin took the brunt of it, sir. He were standing up for us."

It was getting OTT. Maybe the captain was too frustrated to notice. Still, it had passed a little bit of time for him, hadn't it? He'd not have had anything better to do. He had one more try, though, fair play to him.

"Muslims don't drink, either," he said. "Do they?"

"Do we," corrected Shahid, mildly. "No, sir, that's right. Have you studied comparative religion?" He stopped before he went too far. "No, sir," he said. "But we're very good at calling taxis." Pause. "And driving them."

So that was that, then. The officer gave up the fight before he lost his temper with an Asian, and we took the opportunity to slide out of the canteen after him, before Martie could make up his mind to kill Shahid on the spot. We went and found a comfort zone behind the garages and smoked a joint or two.

Sometimes, the army could be almost sweet.

Four

"What d'you do that for, anyway?" I asked Shahid.

"What?" said Shahid, pulling on his toke. "Save his life? You've got to stick together, 'aven't you?"

The sun was shining, and the weed was off of Sambo, and it was really good. We were lying on a patch of concrete behind some sort of shed, and even the grass was steaming, it was that hot. It *was* a sweet life, when you thought about it. Smoking dope just after breakfast in the English countryside, and getting paid for it. By the Queen!

"Oh yeah," I said. "Like in that dump last night. You set him up for that battering, don't deny it."

"But you've got to get your own back somehow, too. I'm a minority, ain't I? I'm downtrodden."

I grinned. I was going to make a dead good point.

"So you're a racist too," I said. "You've just proved it."

He looked at me, and then he smiled.

"I don't hate him 'cause he's white, though, do I? I hate him because he's Corporal Martin."

That made me laugh. I could join this game.

"He's not white anyway," I said. "He's a Scouser. Irish with a bit of English whore mixed in. I hate the Irish, me."

That came out sort of bitter, which it shouldn't have done in actual fact. In actual fact it wasn't even true. I still thought of Bridget – Bridgie – quite a lot. And I didn't really hate her.

"Girl is it?" he said. "You don't know what girl trouble is until you become a Muslim, mate. Don't tell me you're 'ard done by."

I wasn't planning to tell him anything as it happened – I wasn't half pissed for a start off – but it just came out.

"Not much to tell," I said. "She's not even really Irish really, according to her mum and dad. They went to fucking Northern Ireland four hundred fucking years ago from Scotland, and they love the Queen. They're Protestants."

"No shit, Sherlock," said Shahid. "So why d'you hate her, though? What's her name?"

"Bridgie. From Portavogie. The nastiest, meanest, coldest dump I've ever been to, and I had to pay her ferry fare as well, which was bog standard with her. If she had a talent it was chiselling. Tight bitch."

He looked at me down his nose. I couldn't read his thoughts.

"I met her when I did volunteer work in Manchester," I carried on. "Needle exchange. Druggy drop-in for druggy drop-outs. She was one of them, but nearly clean by then. Just a bit of dope, few E's and crap like that, and when I went to uni she sort of tagged along, she shared my student lodgings, like. Bloody nightmare. She was like an anorexic whippet, all pointed knees and elbows, and the bed was two foot wide. Like sleeping with a bunch of butchers' knives."

"Just stop complaining," Shahid said. "I never went to university. Or shagged an Irish girl."

"Not missed a lot," I said. "The sex didn't last for long, and nor did uni, I got kicked out. She started shagging the lads down the passage while I was at me lectures – and they *were* Irish, the real thing, from the south. They played rebel music all night every night, then slept all day and fucked my girlfriend while I went to class. I learnt some good stuff off 'em, though. Guitar tunes, songs. I played a lot, them days. I can't believe it, looking back. I really can't."

The sun went behind the clouds, and it got quite chilly. Good job we were soldiers, eh? Well 'ard. I made a smoking gesture with my mouth and fingers. Time for another one. But Sha was thinking.

"I can't see you as a folkie," he said. "Did you have long hair? Come to think of it, I can't see you at university, neither. What were you in for?"

"You make it sound like bloody prison, mate. Oh, some crappy boring thing, I only did it for my mum, she believed in education, she thought I ought to 'have a chance.' I had the A-levels, I should've got a useful job."

"What, like the army? Ho bleeding ho."

"No, like helping druggies, I enjoyed that, anything. But that's the trouble really, innit, what's a proper job? I mean, you've got to live, and helping people, you don't get paid at all. Fucking peanuts. Fucking disgrace. And by the time I got kicked out of education there weren't no jobs no more and I'd borrowed fucking thousands, and the army was telling great big steaming lies to get us to join up. Like they pay you lots of lovely money. I couldn't believe it when my sister worked it out. It's just above slave fucking labour."

He'd started rolling. He gave the big fat joint a lot of tender care.

"I fell for that as well," he said. "They talked about the minimum wage as if we work a forty hour week. For twenty four hours out of every twenty four, fifty two weeks a year, it's closer to fuck all. Or less maybe. And then they charge us for the stuff we get to eat. Amazing."

The sun came out again, hard and lovely. Shahid lit up and sucked and sighed and thought. Me ditto. Bridgie at the needle exchange when I first met her. What a wreck. Needle exchange! Hola – if those wanks could only see me now.

"What were hers like?" he said suddenly. "Her mum and dad? You said you went to Portathingie?"

"Never met 'em. She'd left me waiting at the harbour because she thought she'd better check 'em out, she hadn't let on I was in the Army. She rang me on me mobile. They were going to kill me if I ever showed me face. End of story."

"Are you winding me up? I thought you said she were a Protestant?"

"Yeah, funny innit? If I'd just been English I'd've been all right, she said. No prejudice in her family, not much! But the Army! I thought she was 'aving me on at first, but she meant it, and she said she'd warned me what a weird dump Portavogie was, the silly cow. The paving stones are all red white and blue, I've never seen so many Union Jacks in all me life, and every wall was painted with a slogan. Fuck the Pope. No surrender. That sort of stuff. Pretty little place apart from that, there were seals in the harbour. It was full of 'em."

He was pulling smoke down deep into his lungs. His eyebrows went up a notch and he stared at me.

"Seals? What *real* seals? They're not English, are they?"

"English? How the fuck should I know, I didn't talk to them!" I got his drift. "Course they're English, they go everywhere, they *swim*." I took the joint off him and had a giant suck. "Anyway, they'd be Irish, wouldn't they? Portafuckingvogieish. There was lots of them, just swimming round. Black faces. Like Ashton and his family at the bleeding seaside. Is Ashton English? You tell me."

It was the dope talking, I guess, but we thought we were pretty bloody funny. And just at that minute, just like in a film, who comes round the corner but Ashton himself. Coincidence or what?

"Yo bruvvas," he said, sticking his palm out and putting on his dimbo whiteboy badass talk. "'Ow it 'angin' wiv yah den mah bwais?" He did it sometimes, especially to officers, because it made them feel like he was getting down with them. He came from Whalley Range, in actual fact, and when he spoke to black mates you couldn't understand a fucking word of it. He was all right, Ashton. He was a laugh.

"Fuck off you nigger cunt," said Shahid. He grabbed the smoke back off me. "We're talking philosophical down here. Did you ever see an English seal?"

"Seal? I never even saw an English leak." He sat down on the grass – softer than the concrete – then jumped up again, wet arse. "Fuck! Why din't you warn me, bastards!"

"They're Welsh," I said. "Leeks. Don't you know nothing, Ashton?"

"These trousers must be Welsh then. Look, stop going on. You fucking stoned or something? Shahid – he's after you. He's going to give you mega shit. He's got Big Dave and Tony and he's going to have your arse. Just thought I'd tell you, okay? Though Christ knows why, you'll only get what's coming to you."

Shahid was lying on his back now, lungs full, smoke dribbling from his mouth and nostrils, happy as a pig in shit. He had the toke held out, but my fingers stopped before I reached it.

"Who? Martie? Why?"

Ashton said it with a look: revenge. It wasn't rocket science.

"He'll have Billy 'Unt onside an' all," he said. "And Bollocks Bowyer. I thought we might take a ride. Lickle trip into the country for our health, like. Know what I mean?"

Shahid laughed so hard he damn near dropped the joint.

"You kill me, Ash," he said. "For our health!"

"Suit yourself," said Ashton. "It's just he's on your case, that's all. He's putting it about all over. You're a monkey, and you've made a monkey out of him. He ain't having it, old son, he's your superior, ain't he? In every way. When Sambo asked him if it were a colour thing, Martie threatened to knock him down. 'I'm superior because of this,' he goes, and sticks his shoulder out, as if his stripe was on his civvie shirt. 'Colour don't come into it, you daft black twat!'"

Shahid giggled.

"What did Wasambu say? Nowt, I bet. Christ, he really is thick that lad, int'e?"

"Nah," said Ashton, "Sambo's not thick, he's up to something, he's working it all out. He'll be the king of Bongo Bongo Land someday, I'd put me arse on it."

I nodded. Sambo wasn't thick, no way. Half the barracks owed him money. He lent it to you, and if you said you didn't have none when he asked for an instalment back, he just smiled.

"Martie's thick," said Ashton. "Did you know he failed the entrance exam for the NF once? Straight up, that. And the BNP and EDL."

"I'm not surprised," said Shahid. "It's a hard exam, that is. Question One, right? What was Hitler's first name?"

"Adolf." Quick as a flash, me.

"It's Heil," said Shahid, expelling smoke from every orifice. "Heil Hitler. Now who knows fuck all?"

"Talk of the devil," said Ashton. "On your feet, lads. He's found us. Shahid – roach!"

It flicked through the air and Ashton trapped it with his foot. Scrudge-scrudge-scrudge into the long wet grass. I whipped my coat off and swung it like a windmill. When Corporal Martin fronted up, the air was clear as crystal. What's more, his face was full of fucking smiles, as if the night before just hadn't happened. Now what the hell was going off?

"Been smoking weed, lads?" (Blank stares all round.) "Should of called me in, I've got some great stuff in me locker. Listen – heard the buzz? There's going to be a rumble tonight, other side of town. The Perokeeto. Our chance to score some big ones. Us against the gippoes. They've been getting uppity."

40

It was a relief to know he'd let us off the hook, but I must admit I felt a sense of gloom and doom, and not just because I thought he might be stringing us along. The sun was out, for fuck sake, the world was looking good, and Corporal Martin, like every other bugger in the army, could only think of trouble. I glanced around and saw that Sha and Ashton felt the same.

"Bloody hell, Lance," I said. "Can't we just chill for once? We had a fight last night, ain't that enough?"

"Beaten by the Banglas," put in Sha, all reasonable-like. "Got to prove it with the gypsies now, have we?"

He had a way with words, did Sha. You could see him digging at Martie's "picking at the sore. And Martie almost fell for it, he had to nearly crack his face to keep up the friendly mask. He was cooking something up. Not pleasant.

"Some of my best friends are gypsies," Ashton said, winking at me on the sly. "They provide a useful service to the black community. They steal unwanted babies."

"They make you lot look good, that's for sure," snapped Corporal Martin. "They're even bigger shit than you are."

"Nice," said Shahid. He made a face at Ashton. "Probably even true."

"Well fuck the lot of you," said Martin, losing his cool. "You're not English anyway, I wouldn't expect you to fucking understand. Or are you yellow? These Pikies have been taking the piss for weeks down here, they shit the place up. They've got a camp down past the ranges, they've been doing things to local girls. They're bleeding animals."

"Probably eat human flesh," said Sha. "I've read about 'em in the Daily Mail."

"There you are then," went Martin. "Fact. And we're going to fucking clear 'em out, tonight. Everybody's in it. The Para-boys are coming in. There's going to be a bloodbath, and we're going to keep our end up. Ain't you ever heard of fucking honour, you fucking toerags? Or don't they have it where you come from?"

"Whalley Range," said Ashton. "Darkest Manchester."

"I'm Oldham me," said Shahid. "Born and bred. Waterloo Street forever, and Limeside can go to hell! That's honour, Corporal. Paki Pride."

I kept my mouth shut, like I always did. Hassan from Blackburn, even if I was completely white. Would you've spoke? Anyway, I thought Mart was going mental, completely ape. But there was three of us, and only one of him. He looked at me and his eyes were like little poison darts.

"You're the fucking traitor," he said. "These two don't know no better, do they? But just remember, Sunshine – you ain't got no protection. We're the fucking minority in this country now."

I didn't have an answer to that one, but Sha was grinning.

"Shit," he said. "You got all the virtues, don't you, Martie?"

"Fuck off you Paki twat! And don't you fucking call me Martie, okay? Never! I'll fucking Agai you! In fact fuck off the lot of you! I'm ashamed to have you in my outfit. I'm ashamed to have you in the British Army. You're finished. All of you. I've marked your fucking cards."

He give us one more poison glare, turned on his heel, and buggered off. Ashton joined us sitting on the concrete, but we none of us relaxed. There was a lot to think about in that.

"What say we go to town and get a curry and a pint?" Ashton said, finally. "Lamb madras for me. Ice cold fucking lager."

"You'd need a vindaloo to get the taste of that twat out of your gob," said Shahid. "Hey, Tiny. Don't you go with no dirty slags tonight, will you?"

I blinked at him. Now what?

"You ain't got no protection, right? The corporal says."

It wasn't very funny, so no one laughed.

Five

With all the pressure off, with pints of lager stood in front of us, and plates of poppadoms and chopped onions and raita while we waited for the stuff to come, we got onto the favourite subject, naturally. For starters, Ashton hadn't had it for twelve hours, maybe more.

"Yeah, but d'you reckon Goughie has?" said Shahid. "I mean, I've met some stupid tarts in my life, but not one stupid enough to go with him like, surely?"

"Oh come on," said Ashton. "There ain't no bird on this earth won't drop her drawers for someone. It depends on the size of your trouser bulge. That's the clincher."

"Bloody hell," I said. "That's Goughie screwed. I've seen his dick, it's bloody near invisible."

"Who's on about his dick?" said Ashton, all innocence. "I meant his friggin' wallet. How do you think rich bastards get the smartest totty, eh? Look at that dwarfy git that runs F1. Look at Piers Morgan, I read somewhere his knob was like a sausage on a stick. Don't stop him using it, does it? Disgusting."

Shahid called the waiter over – in Urdu, or something foreign – and ordered three more beers, then drained the last dregs of his first pint and wiped his hand across his mouth.

"If Johnnie Gough was rich as Richard Branson," he said, "he couldn't get his end away. You're mental, Ash. He married Mrs Hand. He's stuck with her."

We were talking about Goughie because we'd just seen him off. We'd nearly bumped into him in actual fact, down the street on our way to Curry Corner. Every one-horse bastard of a town has got one these days, and you often find the squaddies there, because it's proper grub compared with army shite. He was looking for some company.

"Look out! Look out!" said Ashton, the man with eagle eyes. "It's Billy No-Mates!"

Shahid was in the lead, and he'd narrowed it down to two curry shops where the menu looked okay, he said. He dodged us past the first one, though, because we knew that Gough might've clocked us, and did a sort of double round a crowd of punters and nicked into the second one like lightning. It had a glass front you could see through, but Shahid didn't let that bother him.

"Salamu elei kum!" he gabbled at two waiters, and sort of rushed them before they'd got out their reply. He took us all in in a gesture, pointed through the window, and told them something very quick and fast. They were superstars. No questions asked. We were bucketed through the plastic curtain to the kitchen – which was a first for me – and stood there like arseholes, wreathed in smiles. Two cooks, two waiters, all skinny Paki men, all half discomknockerated. We smiled, they didn't, till one of the two who'd led us in did some explanations (or said some bloody thing, in any case). And Shahid pulled the plastic beads aside, stared out for a few seconds, then spread his hands out like an Eastern lord.

"Thanks, lads," he told them. "I'll do the same for you next time you're up in Rusholme! Come on boys, let's eat."

Speculating on the size of Goughie's todger didn't keep our interest very long, but we stayed with the subject, naturally. Ashton, who was so keen on it he was even getting married, always wanted to talk about anybody else's sex life, especially Shahid's, which I thought was sort of weird meself. But when Sha asked him why he wanted to know, he didn't even understand the question.

"What d'you mean, why?" he said. "Why d'you think? I've never talked about it to a Paki, have I, I don't fucking know none. Bloody 'ell mate, where I come from we're not exactly mates, are we, and to us your birds are bloody Daleks, walking binbags with a slitty little eyehole. I feel sorry for 'em, like, but I'd never get to screw one, would I? I mean, what do they wear underneath, for instance? They don't go bollock naked, surely!"

The waiters came up then and started dishing out, so Sha clammed up. He smiled at them and nodded, and he thanked them as every plate went down, although I guess that they were Banglas and he hated them.

"Come on," said Ashton, when they went away. "Do they wear bras and knickers? Thongs? G-strings? Bloody hell! Aladdin's cave!"

Shahid filled his face with curry.

"How should I know," he said at last. "I'm a Muslim, ain't I? I respect women. I'm not an oversexed black monkey."

Ashton was disappointed.

"Respect my arse," he went. "You telling me that Asian crumpet don't? Because I don't believe you, mate, no way. Anyway, you got sisters. You must've seen what they wear under 'em."

"I'm not a pervert, either," Shahid said. "And anyway, I don't see my sisters any more, do I, I'm in the army. At the risk of sounding racist, I'm the black sheep. Shorn. Cut off without a bleeding penny. Even visiting our house I'd be safer with a rifle in me hand these days."

"Bloody hell," said Ashton. "Just in case you want to cop a look?" I think he was joking, but if he was it didn't work.

"Did you do something bad or something, Sha?" I asked. "To get cut off, like, or was it just the army bit? Why did the family go against you?"

"Islam means submission," he said. "I didn't fancy it. I'd seen a bit too fucking much of it, growing up. I loved my sisters. Plus I've got two brothers and I hate them."

"Bloody hell," I said. "Happy Families."

"You don't know the fucking half of it," he said. "One sister…"
He stopped. "Well, let's just say she's as mental as the rest of them.
Submission, see? It's total fucking bollocks."

"But you said it's the same word," said Ashton, triumphantly. "See!
I got you there! So Islam's fucking bollocks!"

I'm not religious myself, not in any way, but this all sounded wrong
to me, it sounded…well…disloyal or something. I mean, would I say
that Christians were all mental? Catholics? Well, obviously I would,
they are. But for a Paki – somehow it seemed different. Frightening.

"Fuck," said Ashton, when Shahid didn't take the challenge.
"You've got it bad, mate. You can't hate 'em enough to want to
kill 'em, though, so why join the fucking army? One madhouse to
another that is, how much sanity do you see round here? Martie
Martin? Bollocks Bowyer and Billy 'Unt? You must be joking."

Sha wiped his plate down with a bit of naan. He stuffed it in and
swallowed, a great big lump. Like he was trying not to say no more
or something.

"There's mad and mad," he said, at last. "I got forced down to the
mosque after school for years and bleeding years, chanting Arabic
out of the Koran, the Q'ran as they call it now, can you hear the difference? The bloke that 'taught' me was an old prat from the wilds
of fucking nowhere, could hardly speak a word of English, who told
us that we had to hate you lot, the *kuffar*, because you're unbelievers
in a godless country. Godless! Well, I was bloody *born* here."

He looked a bit upset, maybe, so I thought I'd try and lighten it.

"Well, he's dead right there," I said, "we're unbelievers, that's for sure. I mean, England's a Christian country, spose to be, but I don't know anyone who actually believes the crap. I mean, it's Stone Age, bollocks, we just go along with it to save the sweat. Bloody hell, even you go to church parades, don't you? Beats working, any day."

Shahid finished off his pint, and his eyes cleared slowly.

"Yeah," he said, "and that's the bastard, innit? Stone Age bollocks, dreamed up by some fucking madman in a fucking cave, unbeliev-able. And we believe in it and you've grown out of it, we need another hundred years. I believe it too, in some sort of stupid, gutless way, I just can't shake it. Bred in the fucking bone."

"Once a Catholic always a Catholic, that's what my Auntie Ellen says," said Ashton, brightly, then thought he must have got it wrong. "What? What's wrong with that?"

"Nowt," said Sha. "You've hit it, Ashton, really. We're a lot like Catholics, except we kill each other instead of wasting time with arguing. Sunni, Shia, Sufi, Wahhabi – each gang of them thinks their gang's got it right and old Allah says the others must be killed, it's only justice because he told them personal. And the good thing is, when us Brits invaded it made it all our fault, they can kill us now in any country in the world. Blow up a hundred Muslims watching the world cup? Best news a Muslim's ever heard, and that's official from Al Qaida. And we're to blame. It's marvellous."

We, you, him, them – it was too complicated for Ashton, and me as well if I'm being honest. But my glass was empty, so I put me hand up for a waiter, and signalled three. He nodded. The universal language of the pisshead.

"We've got it right on one thing, though," said Ashton. "They'll kill anyone, your lot. I've studied it. I've read it in the Sun. No duff information there!"

"Yeah, and that's your trouble," said Shahid. "As a race, society, whatever. You know Jack Shit. Jack Shit about fuck all. All Jocks are mean, all Scousers thieve, French girls are all sexy, politicians all tell lies, and single mums all scrounge. So Muslims are all terrorists. It stands to fucking reason."

"Well this bit does," said Ashton comfortably. "All terrorists are Muslims. Now that you *can't* deny, can you?"

"And I'm a Muslim in the British Army. Maybe that's why I joined up in the first place, to show you it's not true." Sha paused, as if he was thinking. "Or to show kids in the places I grew up that there were other ways. You can try to do things right and be a Muslim."

"You're not a Muslim, mate," crowed Ashton. "You're a fucking traitor, I bet that's what your family think. Fact is you couldn't get another fucking job, just like the rest of us, and bollocks to Allah! Deny it, wanker, I dare you to deny it. Bollocks to Allah!"

The new beer was arriving, and the waiter spilled some on to the table, where it ran off on to Shahid's leg. They both pretended to ignore it, but I thought I'd better change the subject off religion smartish. And terrorism, come to that. The trouble was, my mind was nearly blank.

"What did they say, though? Shahid? When you joined? Did they mind?"

He stared for a moment, as if he didn't get the question. The waiter went off, but didn't take the plates away.

"My father beat me up," he said. His eyes turned inwards, like he was looking inside his head. He made a grimace with his lips. "The brothers brought some friends in from the mosque, they all joined in, they said it were an honour thing, I'd invited shame on the community. Honour. It's a good word, innit?"

Ashton wasn't listening. He made a noise and I followed his eyes to the window. A face. Pale and stupid, pressed up against the glass just like a kid.

"Shit," said Ashton. "Rumbled. Get us out of *this* one, Shahid!"

Sha looked up.

"Good," he said. "Talking of honour, here's our meal ticket. And it means we can't come back again. The waiter's fucking crap."

He'd lost the both of us this time, but he didn't bother to explain. He watched the door open and he greeted Goughie like a long lost pal. Gough didn't even look suspicious.

"Hi, lads. Thought I saw you earlier. What you doing?"

51

"On-line poker," said Ashton, not too unpleasantly. "Can't you see, you twat?"

"You eating?" asked Sha. "Grub's good, mate. Get us another beer, we'll sit with you."

Now what's going on, I thought. If I had much more beer I'd bleeding burst. Crap and a kip, that would be my recipe for a quiet afternoon. Maybe some movie. Shahid couldn't mean it, surely?

"Oh!" said Goughie. He was surprised, but looked dead pleased. "Yeah. What a good idea. What's the prices like?"

"Rock bottom. Cheap as chips. Tell the lad I sent you. Abdul, that's his name, I think. He's a Catholic."

"You what? *Catholic?*"

Me and Ashton caught each other's eyes, but we didn't laugh. *Catholic*. What was the bastard on about?

"Aye," said Shahid. "Doesn't talk about it much, but you can worm it out of him. Hey!" He called across and said a lot of Asian stuff, and the waiter looked amazed. But he clocked onto Goughie's face, then said, "Okay."

"Go on," said Sha. "Get us three more beers and give the lad your order. Just don't tell him we're army, okay? It won't go down too well."

Gough hesitated – who wouldn't – but Shahid sort of pushed him forward, smiling fit to bust.

"The dupiaza's good," he said. "Ain't it, Tiny? Just as good as mother used to make it!"

In half a minute Gough was deep in conversation with the waiter, buried in a menu while Abdul poured the pints. Shahid reached across the table and shoved us all towards the door.

"What?" said Ashton. "What the fuck—?"

"Shut up you fool," Sha whispered. "Out! Out! Out!"

"But we haven't paid!" I said. "Christ, Shahid!"

"It's down to Goughie," Sha whispered. "I've told the waiter it's his treat. Quick, before the bugger notices!"

He made it to the door like silent lightning, and me and Ashton were a second later. The waiter saw us go, but I guess Sha's story covered that 'cause he didn't shout or nothing. Out in the street Sha and Ash were into mega-giggles.

"Your face, Tiny!" Ashton said. "Don't you like free food or summat? Hey, bloody Goughie! Like taking ice cream off a kid!"

"It's the principle, not the cash," said Sha, as if I'd understand. "He'll be okay, he's got nowt else to spend his money on, has he? Anyway, it's that fucking waiter I was after, not old Gough. He messed my trackies up, the Bangla get, and did he apologise? Nah – because it were done on purpose, weren't it? I weren't going to pay in any case. Just this way, Goughie gets to take the flak!"

We'd made about a hundred metres from the cafe when there was a big commotion down the road behind us. The door had slammed open and Johnny Gough was out, cork from out a champagne bottle, running like fuck. Away from us, luckily, and chased by three Pakis (or Bangla-men, let's get it right!). Chinese waiters in a suchlike situation carry knives and cleavers, that's a well-known fact, but this lot at least appeared to be unarmed. And Gough was fast, fair play to him. He was a champion!

"Shit, look at Goughie go!" said Ashton.

"I never thought he had it in him," said Shahid. "We ought to go back in and smash the dump up to show him some appreciation."

"Nick the till," said Ashton. "Take a contribution for the trouble they've put us through."

"Especially Goughie," said Shahid. "He didn't even get a curry and a pint of piss. Shall we follow on and see what happens?"

We didn't, though. We found a quiet spot down by the river and smoked a bit of shit. I kipped a bit, Ashton watched the girls and played a bit of pocket billiards, and Shahid did a bit of thinking.

Leastways, that's what he said he did. His final conclusion, apparently, was that we should go to the nightclub later and suss out the
gippo thing.

"It's the best thing about the army really," he said. "You can always
guarantee a fight if you look hard enough. I wonder if Goughie'll
come. Hope so."

"You what?" I said. "Why?"

He laughed.

"He's got potential," he said. "He's just took on half of Sylhet
single-handed, saved me the bother. If I'm not careful, I'll have to
talk to him. Make him a friend."

"Christ," said Ashton, as if he was suddenly deeply interested. He
was.

"Look at the tits on that," he said, pointing across the grass. "World
fucking class..."

Six

You could tell that it was brewing from the start. We didn't kill ourselves to get there and we walked again, which seemed a good plan at the time and was mainly down to Ashton. He liked to check out the local females, he said, and upset them with what they were missing. Shahid said he just liked to shake his gonads down, which Ash quite liked when Sha explained what gonads were.

In fact, he asked Sha how he knew so much stuff, big words and so on, and Shahid laughed.

"Ask Tiny, not me, mate," he said. "He went to university, which in Blackburn terms makes him an aristocrat, first class. He's the big words king."

"Balls," I said. "I don't even know what one of them is. An errister-what?"

"Got you there, Sha!" Ashton crowed. "You're a stuck-up twat, I always knew it. I bet you could've gone. Too bloody idle, were you?"

Shahid wasn't fazed. Why should he be? We were strolling on a quiet afternoon, still warm although the sun was nearly gone, no work to do till Monday and the world our bleeding oyster.

"It were me dad's decision, nowt to do with me," he said. "When my teachers told him I should try for uni he lost his English, didn't he? That's the best thing about bilingualism. You can forget which one you're meant to know, any time you fancy."

"Bi what?" said Ashton. "You mean your old man goes with blokes?"

"Ho bloody ho," said Shahid. "He's not even bilingual, come to think of it, his English is diabolical. But when the school sent a translator he couldn't speak Urdu neither. Or Bengali, Hindi, double-Dutch, you name it. It saved him thousands on me fees, and the translators are paid for on the rates. This fucking country's mad."

Comes to something when your Paki mates sound like the BNP, but I let it go. I was trying to keep the heat off me.

"So you'd have gone as well if he'd let you, right?" I said. "So why you tearing the piss out of me? A year at uni, failed, don't make you a middle-class wanker, you know."

"So here's the difference," said Shahid. "Your mum's skint okay, but she sent you despite of it, and my dad could've sent me free but couldn't see the point. 'No bloody thank you, Mr Britain – here's my nose, watch me while I cut it off to spite my face.'" He paused, briefly. "You should have stuck it, mate. I would've done. Or haven't you noticed where you've ended up?"

We all laughed at that, but it didn't feel so funny, really. For a moment I was tempted to tell 'em I'd only joined when I was desperate, and because the lying bleeding adverts said that I could learn a trade like brickeying or carpentry or plumbing, but I didn't want to go there, it pissed me off too much to even think of it. I pushed Ashton into a pub instead, where I'd seen some totty peering through the window, and by the time we got to the Perokeeto, we were pretty well oiled and we had four exotic birds in tow (English country style!) to put the tin lid on it.

Exotic? Jesus! They were completely mental, and as ugly as an American evangelist. Ashton's Talking Dogs, Shahid called them to their faces, but they didn't mind, they needed "male escorts" to get in, that was the Perokeeto rule. They nearly talked our tits off in the pub, and they made me miss Bridgie, to be quite honest, because she was too miserable to talk at all most of the time. They were okay though, not after owt, and it kept up the essential blood-flow in Ashton's keks.

It was information that we needed, more than anything, and they were pretty hot on that once we'd got them going, although they had the cheek for starters to ask me if I was a pikey, which made the others fall about. I've never been a tidy sort of guy, but for fuck sake! Then they said it was a joke, of course, and clinched it by saying that the barman didn't serve gippoes in any case, so I must be all right. Anyway, said the funniest one, who was called Becks, pikies didn't pal out with blacks and Pakis, did they? Even pikies had their standards!

I told you they were mental. They could've got their heads kicked in for that sort of talk, but Sha and Ashton played along as if it was the height of wit. And now the conversation was round to gypsies, Sha kept it there. He should have been a lawyer, really. He was made for it.

It turned out there was a gypsy camp about a mile away, and they'd been coming in and causing shit for ages. The girlies squabbled for a while if they were really gypsies, or "travellers," or "diddycoys" (that's what it sounded like), and with their crazy country accents it was quite a bit of fun. Anyway, they said, they were bloody 'orrible, and filthy, and they'd turned the place into "a praaper slum." They chucked their rubbish over the hedges into the fields and road, they didn't have lavatories, they spread disease ("it stands to reason, dunnit?"), and they all drove "Mercedeezeez and Beemurrz" and lived off the Social – special pikey rates, 'undreds and 'undreds of quid a week. And they all had fifteen children and a dog.

"They smash the pubs up, too," said Clare. "They're all banned, innay? They go in the lavvies and shit straight on the floor. And then they don't use paper! They're animals!"

"Why would they do that?" said Shahid, keeping a straight face. "Do they like getting shit up their fingernails to have a sniff at later? Or is it nice and squidgy for their toes?"

"Don't you be so daft!" said Clare. "They paags, is what. They just durty paags!"

"Paags?" said Shahid. "Bloody Nora, what's a paag when it's at home?"

"You should know!" said Becks, bright as a button. "Them things you Pakis ain't allowed to eat. Oinkers. 'Ogs. *You* know!"

"'E's takin' the piss," said Ally. "'Tent funny, matey, 'tis serious! They rapin' girls now! They stealin' knickers off of lines! When they were over in 'Ampshire near my aunty's 'ouse a little baby disappeared!"

We were in Ashton's territory now. The rest of it he hadn't bothered with. Probably heard it all before about his family, back in Manchester.

"Told you, lads," he said. "Baby stealing, well-known fact. Fuck that though, you can always get more babies, what's this about rape, that's much more interesting. Have any of you lot been done? Or don't you fancy that sort of thing?"

"It's true!" said Clare, completely scandalised. "Tell 'im, Leigh-Ann. You knew a girl, din't you? She knew a girl! She did!"

Leigh-Ann was the quiet one, but she managed not to blush.

"Thass right. Me cousin's mate. I even know 'er name if I could remember it. Sarah... Sasha... no, summink like that. Oh it was terrible. In hospital for months, she was. Turned her nearly inside out they did."

"Ten of 'em!" said Clare. "Thass what I 'eard!"

"Nah," said Becks, the voice of reason. "Four. Five, top whack."

"Ten," said Clare. "It was in the Gazette. Ten of 'em at least!"

"Rosy, that was her name," said Leigh-Ann, suddenly. "I knew it was something like that. Rosy."

"Nah," said Ally. "Rosy Baines got knocked down by a lorry, that's why she was in the paper. Stupid cow."

"That's a different Rosy," said Leigh-Ann, sulkily. "'Ow would you know, anyway? She was my mate, not yourn."

We listened till we got dead bored, and then we took them to the club, like we'd agreed. They still hadn't asked us for anything, not even snout, which was amazing, but they'd filled us in on "all the useful local facts" as Shahid put it, laughing his socks off. In fact we weren't even sure that there were really any gypsies until we turned the last corner to the club. And yeah, there were. Lots of them. And local lads with turnips in their hair. And squaddies. Nothing going off yet, but you could see it was going to be a lively night. Tasty.

It had potential. Shitloads!

Seven

Like every army town I've ever been in, this one was pretty weird. It's as if the people aren't all there, really, they're sort of inbred or something. If Catterick's famous for anything, they tell you when you get there, it's famous for a shit night out. This one was Catterick only more so. Strung out along a long dank country road, with fields all round where the locals only went to shag their favourite sheep or bury babies. The lively end, where we'd been at last night, had cafes, discos, dance halls, bowling – and was about as lively as a frozen turd. This end had the Perokeeto.

From the outside it looked like what it was – an old-style cinema that had gone under when the multis had come in. Not that there was a multi, even at the jumpin' end of town (joke, by the way) 'cause we'd thought we might grab a movie earlier, until we asked. The only reason it was here at all was that this end also had the off-road training base and the small-arms and hand-to-hand combat ranges, so lots of squaddies spent lots of time here, in a sort of separate barracks area. Naturally, the army hadn't thought about what they could do for pleasure – the army never does. It's a funny thing I learned quite fast when I joined up – they never learn.

Thousands and thousands of blokes, mainly led by halfwits, who work and train and run and harden up, and once they've reached a certain point of fitness and frustration, get given time off with fuck all to do. There's sport, of course, and there's daytime TV and Playstations and Wii. There's evenings off and most weekends, and the local slags to help you enjoy it. Army town slags. Boggin'. 'Angin'. The only ones worth screwing are married – the army wives – and that can get you into trouble. The rest are your Leigh-Anns and Allys, who I wouldn't touch with yours, mate, let alone me own. Two pubs down this end. Two pubs and one so-called nightclub. The bleeding Perokeeto.

Another thing about army town women, is they'll go with anyone at all, and they've got some kind of death wish. That's where the pikies come in, if you think about it. I mean, I've got nowt against them, because I've never talked to one, they've never done me any harm. I've seen their shitty camps, with their shitty women and their shitty kids, and quite honestly I don't believe it when people tell me they're loaded, because if they were they wouldn't live the way they do, would they? They're just poor dumb bastards who stick together with their bloody dogs to keep off rubberneckers and the council, and they get kicked around from place to place like sacks of useless crap. No woman in her right mind would go near any of the men – ratty little Irish bastards with ferret's eyes, most of 'em – and them that do are slags, aren't they? You could see the pikies outside the Perokeeto, and you could see the local girls. You could see the trouble hanging in the evening air.

"Why do they do it?" I said. Jesus, I was feeling philosophical. "Why do they fucking do it?"

I didn't mean just our girls, who'd left us now we'd got them in, thank God. I meant all the rest of them as well, including Ashton, who'd been absorbed into the crowd, who'd gone off sniffing like a dog on heat for anything worth hunting. The place was like a swamp, a throbbing, heaving jungle of bass and drums, with flashing lights and a roar of shouted talk that almost matched the music.

"Because they want a life!" roared Shahid, close to my head. "They're desperate. I'm desperate for a drink, an' all. Shall we get some E's?"

"Lager!" I shouted back. "Fuck E's. If there's going to be a punch-up, I don't want to have a smile stuck on me face, do I? That way you get a fist through it!"

The rush at the bar was horrendous, and the aggression was already building up. It's as if they do it on purpose – not enough people serving, not enough space to cram the punters in. Lager squirted out of plastic hosepipes, never a glass filled to the top, no time or room to check your change. Then every now and then the shriek of girls when they find out how much the bastards are charging for a bottle of water – more than bloody Scotch. I checked out later in the toilets when I went for a slash, and there were no taps either. Take ecstasy, take water, even garrison slags know that. So do the Perokeeto owners, obviously. Ah well. Dead girls must be good publicity in this one horse burg, maybe.

The other incredible thing was they were letting gippoes in. Great rules they had on the door in this place – no girls without a bloke, no bottles, no lads already pissed. But in came the pikies, all brown and slinky-eyed. Race thing, Shahid called it. They had to let him in, and even scum like Ashton, and the gippoes could call the cops on the same basis. "Oh please, sir, it's me human rights! It's the race relations act!" And as they'd come for trouble, because they liked a fight as much as drunken squaddies do, they were probably tooled up as well. Forward planning. When it kicked off, it would really kick off good.

We went for a wander when we'd got our pints, because all in all there was damn all else to do. We all liked dancing when the time was right, who doesn't? But the time wasn't right tonight, it was farcical. Ninety per cent of the people on the floor were female, dancing round their handbags like Blackburn in the old days, only not so well-dressed. All the wall space was jammed with blokes, all holding pints in plastic glasses, all glaring at the dancers as if they wished they'd die. And glaring at each other, in the flashing gloom, sizing up who was sizing them up, and where the fighting would break out.

Shahid shouted something in my ear. I couldn't hear him. There was beer and curry on his breath when he bawled again. That was close enough.

"Look! Over there! It's Goughie!"

Ashton – back from his crumpet count ("minus bugger all worth shagging") – nudged me from the other side.

"Sod Gough!" he yelled, "Look over there! The Colour Sergeant! And there's that SAS man! Christ, it's big boys' fun tonight!"

The Colour Sergeant was a real big shock, because people of his rank don't mix with us scum, hardly ever. Within two minutes I'd clocked two other sergeants, and then the CSM! Jesus H. Christ! Serious!

"What SAS man?" Shahid roared. "What you on about?"

Ashton and me exchanged a look. Quite good that Sha didn't know everything, after all. We'd talked to this guy in the bar at camp one night. He spoke like an officer, but he was all right.

"Him!" I said. "Ginger hair! He's only with us for the cover. He works in Kosovo in plain clothes. Sort of spy."

Shahid looked at me as if I'd gone mental. Miffed because he didn't know, I guess. Ashton caught the look.

"Oh fuck off, Stan, you don't know everything. Listen. He's got ginger hair, but no one takes the piss, *no*body. That makes him mega, okay? Just fucking think about it, you stuck up bastard."

But Shahid had lost interest. He'd clocked someone else.

"Mart!" he said. "Over by that pillar. And Bollocks and Big Dave. Christ, Mart's black eye's come out all right, ain't it? Like a rotten plum."

"Well, it were him what told us there'd be a kick-off," I said. "Course he's here, it stands to reason. Steer clear, I reckon. He'll get us too, give him half a chance if there's a riot."

"I ain't scared of Martin," Shahid began, but Ash had picked out some others in the click – Chas Hicks and Geordie George. They were in the druggies' corner, naturally, and Josh P would be there somewhere. In the gents maybe, shooting up. Then I saw Billy 'Unt and Timmo Hawes, which just left Sambo. Who had more sense, in my opinion. You don't get to be dictator of Bongoland mixing in crap like this.

We just stood there for a while, like. Spare pricks at a wedding, more or less. Observers, maybe – that sounded better, didn't it? We watched Martie trying to grease up to the Colour and the CSM, and they didn't fuck him off, which was bad news. They were gathering a team.

"I wonder why they're bothering," said Sha. "I mean, they don't need these nasty little scrubbers to hang around with, do they? Why should they care if the gippoes want to give them HIV?"

"Ooh!" said Ashton. "Anal! I like that."

"Anyway, where are they?" Sha went on. "The pikies? You white bastards all look the same to me! Let's have another pint. I'm going to put a Scotch in mine. Two. It's Saturday, lads. Where's the fucking *buzz*?"

The crowd were swirling now, but certainly I hadn't seen no bloodshed, or even moves towards it. But as we drifted off to get the booze, I did see Corporal Mart again, and he'd seen us. He was tracking through the dancers like a gundog. More like a big brown bear, in fact. With a sore head.

"Wanker watch!" I said. "He's after us. Melt-melt-melt!"

Fat chance in this crush. He saw us trying to evade and he threaded faster. He kicked some girl's handbag and she swore at him (we couldn't hear it, obviously) and he swore back and made a lovely sign. A bloke nearby sort of lunged at him – you leave my slag alone, even if I've never met her in my life before – but Martie jerked away and bashed on in our direction, saving himself for later would be my guess.

"Ere! Slags!" he shouted, when he was near enough. "Where the fuck've you been hiding? There's going to be trouble, and we're in with the CSM, I've volunteered us. Clear-out time for pikey rapists. The Final Solution. And there'll be drinks in it, he's well made up."

"We've got our own," I said. "We're on our way for top-ups now."

"Fuck that!" said Martin. "Booze afterwards. It's getting to the point!"

"We'll be with you, Martie!" yelled Ash. "You brown-nose bastard." (That bit was lower, nearly in a normal voice, nearly in my ear'ole.) He shouted again, top-level: "Sorry, can I call you Mart? Are Shahid's sins forgiven?"

He loved to push his luck, did Ashton, but Mart didn't remember we'd "betrayed" him, probably. Leastways, before he could speak, or even put his brain into the proper gear, it was too late. There was a terrific burst of girlie screaming from across the hall, and a sort of surge around the edges that bulged the drinkers into the dance floor, knocking the ladies into their bags and each other's arms and legs. Ashton even managed to get a flash of fanny in the midst of it, he told me later. Mental.

"Oi-oi!" said the Lance. "Chocks away! Come on you bastards! The Skulls forever!"

You what, I thought. You fucking *what*? Who in the name of bollocks were the Skulls?

It wasn't the big kick-off yet, but it was starting. Mart shot off towards the CSM and mates, and Shahid, then Ash, bashed after him. I got lost in a mass of screaming totty – running for the bar and lavatories, the two most important places when you think about it – and I din't try to fight clear. The kick-off end was getting frantic, and I saw two pikies and three squaddies throw themselves through the air and get into the ruck. I also saw a pint beer glass flashing and flying through the light-show like in a magic trick, half-full and upright, not spilling a drop. It landed on the back of some girl's head – only plastic so hardly fatal – but she let out a shriek I heard from twenty feet away. The beer poured down her face and neck in gushes, and she must have thought her brain was pissing blood.

There was a screech through the loudspeakers as the DJ scarred his vinyls, and his voice came on all shaky in a shout. "Calm down, please! Calm down everybody! The police are on their way!"

Then, like a prat, he put the music on again, and it was drowned out by a gigantic roar. Oh God, that lovely word, "police." Now there'd be some fun. The bloodbath could commence.

I'd had enough, I must say. I've never really gone in for this sort of thing, and I wanted out, I had no taste for it. The rush towards the door was getting bigger and more violent, and the floor was full of screamers now, girls who'd been separated from their mates and handbags, some on their hands and knees, some jumping over them, all deadly heels and tree trunk country legs in stripes and glitter. There was a flanking movement over to my right where Martie and my mates had gone, but I kept my face the other way in case Mart or some other bastard eyeballed me. I wondered, not for the first time, if I really wasn't cut out for the army. Maybe I was fucking gay!

By the time I reached the door there was all hell breaking out, pandemonium. The music had stopped for good, the screams were almost constant, and it was only the flashing lights that still told you it was party time. I liked that. A bloodbath breaking out and the wankers couldn't even get round to turning the main lights on. Then they did, as I pushed out into the lobby. I looked back into a sea of seething bodies, everybody slugging everybody else and the tarts darting about like overweight butterflies. Some of them could swing a handbag though. I saw a couple of right good shots go in.

The bouncers looked at me a bit bemused when I went to get out into the street, because there were still masses trying to burst in, blokes *and* girls. The tannoy was booming all over everything, but you couldn't hear a single word, you never can, can you, it's part of the tradition, part of what us English do so well. I often wondered if we'd be any different when we were actually at the war, when we were actually being shot at and bombed out in the East. I doubted it. More and more I fucking doubted it. Like them bombings down the Smoke. The police radios wouldn't work underground, like everyone had told the government year after fucking year, so they tried mobile phones, till some top genius closed the network down because it was too busy, and got promoted! Forward planning.

It was quite nice out in the street when I got clear. There were lots of punters there already, and the ruck was going to spread from inside to out, no danger, pretty soon. But for now it was just gangs of eager lads, gangs of totty tottering on their heels, and lurking gangs of pikies wondering if they were the heroes or the villains. Traffic still running, not a cop in sight despite what the DJ had said, and a smell of frying onions from a burger van. Mm, I thought – burger. No, I thought, too close to the seat of the fire. We'd passed a pizza place further down the road. I'd go and get a pizza and a tin of Coke.

Big shock when I got there though. Halfway along the line of customers, there was bloody Goughie! He must have got out of the punch-up even quicker than I had, which made me feel a wee bit queasy. I mean, I'd left for clever reasons, I couldn't see the point of it, quite honestly. But Goughie was a wimp, a nonce, a wanker. He'd get called a yellow bastard if they found out he'd run. So where did that leave me?

Time to split. I didn't need no pizza anyway. And he turned and saw me, and his face took on a look that said it all – scum of the earth. My stomach sort of dropped, but I might have even blushed as well, I really had felt bad about the way we'd thrown him to the wolves down at the curry place. I sort of coughed.

"You got away okay, then? From them Paki lunatics? That's all right then, eh?"

He had a funny face, Gough. Sort of long and pale, and spotty. No bruises, though. He didn't smile.

"No thanks to you lot. Your idea of pals, was it? Your idea of how to treat a mucker from the mob?"

"It was Shahid, really," I mumbled. Then I felt *really* like a traitor. Christ, Gough was nowt to me. He was a pillock. Prat.

"What a twat," he said. "Too tight to pay for his own fucking curry, is he?"

"You'd be surprised," I said. "In actual fact he thought you'd be... well, he knew you'd get away okay. He was dead impressed."

Sound stupid enough? It did to me.

"Anyway," I said, more aggressively, "what you moaning on about? It was a laugh, that's all. We waited for you down the street. Thought you'd catch up later."

"He's a Paki twat," said Goughie. "And that other one's a cunt-struck coon. I never thought much of you anyway, but when you took up with that lot I knew the lads was right. You're a nigger-lover. Or is that a touch of the tar-brush round your eyes? Hassan, eh? Hassan, is that your problem?"

I'd seen Gough bullied till he nearly died. I'd seen him go through six months of pure fucking hell in training, and I'd sort of sympathi-sed – no, I *had*. I'd even tried to help him once, when the corporals had beasted him in the showers with buckets of cold piss and rubbed shit into his cheeks like L'Oréal (because he was worth it, yes you get the picture), and I'd felt really pissed off with the stunt we'd played him at the curry shop, I'd damn nearly told him we were out of order. But suddenly I'd found out why it happened. For half a second I felt like smacking in his face, his pasty, sneering, wanky little face. We were in a line of people queuing at the till, and they were watching us. One woman had two little kids in tow and I realised she was terrified. It hit me.

But I'd not done anything. We were just talking to each other, separated by these punters waiting for a snack. And I was enraged, I was going to jump him, I'd felt a great black wave of fury, roaring out of nowhere. I saw this woman's face, and then it hit me.

"That's very nice that is," I said. I almost killed myself, to get control. I thought I might be sick. "That's great that is, Goughie, that's fucking brilliant. Why don't you go away before I lose my temper? *Now!* There's children."

The lady's face was like a picture. Goughie, who'd gone pale and tense, was startled too. Christ knows what he was thinking. Christ knows if he *wanted* a fight, I haven't got a frigging clue. All of a sudden he turned, kind of twisted on his heels, jinking sideways. He walked straight past me to the street, and his face was sort of churning. I smiled at the lady, but she didn't smile at me. The lad behind the counter asked her for her order, but suddenly she didn't want to buy. She grabbed the children and bundled them around and away from her, off towards the door. When they made noises she hissed at them, like a snake, it even frightened me. An older lady tutted. She looked at me with pure venom in her eyes, as if I'd done something, as if I was going to murder her, and she wasn't afraid of *me*, no fucking way! And I'd done nothing. *Nothing!* I hadn't done a bleeding thing.

I didn't want a pizza now, but I couldn't let them see that, could I? So I ordered and waited, and I tried not to watch people watching me, and I tried not to *feel* embarrassed, let alone *be* it. I queued, I paid, I got me pizza and I went out into the street and turned my back on the road leading to the Perokeeto and I thought I'd walk away from it. All of it. The lot. I was up to fucking *here* with it, the whole damn boiling.

You can't ignore the sirens though, can you? Even Goughie couldn't, because when I got back towards there I saw him standing on the fringes, looking in. It was like a magnet, and people were coming in from far and wide, they were coming out of the wood-work like creepy-crawlies. It was like the Roman circus, in that film.

The fight had come out of the Perokeeto, and it was washing across the roads and pavements like a tide of dirty surf. No one was in uniform, but you could tell the squaddies from a mile off, or I could, anyway. Everyone was tanked up, pissed as arseholes, but we're still the fittest, by a long shot. You could tell us by the way we ran, and did long sideways kicks up in the air, both feet in, three foot off the ground. You could tell us by the punches, and some of the killer judo jabs the lads were using. Not official training, but everyone gets to know them, you've got to if you want to live. In fact, if it hadn't been for the fact that we *were* all tanked there'd have been some dead'uns, I would judge. People never realise that, when they sound off about "drink-fuelled mayhem." Pissed punches usually don't do much real harm. What do reporters fucking know about drinking? It's a life-saver.

I hadn't really realised I was pissed myself, but as the adrenaline shot through my blood I felt sick again, it got me in a wave. It stopped me rushing in, and it made me want to heave. I'd been at it for nearly twenty-four hours in a way, except for when I was actually asleep, and me legs felt like lead with weights on for a moment. My mouth went dry, and I spat out a bit of pizza and chucked the rest away. The moment passed and I stood back to watch. Still felt shaky though. I needed Scotch or something. I needed to chuck up.

It was a fucking riot, no argument. More and more blokes poured out of the Perokeeto, some to fight in the open, some to escape, who knows? But if they thought they'd find some peace outside they'd got it wrong, big style. Anyone who hadn't found a target yet jumped on them like Homer on a doughnut, and anyone who was getting bored with kicking shit out of some half-dead corpse went for a bit of fresh. The weak and beaten stumbled into the new boys, lambs to the slaughter, to get another battering, and the tide of new blood made it harder to break free of the crowd. In fact in one surge, there were so many on the pavement that half a dozen got pushed up against a shop window till it smashed inwards. You could see them fighting inside, among the granny knitwear, some with bloody great big glass daggers. Cool.

The sirens took a damn long time in coming, they had a hard time getting through in any case. This one-horse end of town had just the one main road, and by now it was pretty solid with jammed-up traffic and fighting blokes and screaming totty. And blood and broken glass and abandoned shoes and handbags, ditto. A couple of young hopefuls of the pikey persuasion were systematically upending them to look for money, and snatching others off of crying girls as well. And being kicked and cursed and monstered for their trouble. Oh, Saturday nights. Don't you just love 'em?

It couldn't last, though, could it? I'd moved up to Gough by now – solidarity, who knows? – and though we didn't talk we felt like older, wiser brothers for a moment. He pointed out our CSM, whose face was streaming blood and who looked so happy you would not believe it. Then we did a pick-parade of lads we knew, and there were tons of them. Geordie George booting someone's head in on the ground, Timmo Hawes getting one right in the bollocks, then Corporal Martin swinging a lump of wood at some young gypsy guy and missing, typical. Then suddenly I saw Sha and Ashton, and they saw us as well. They burst through the crowd towards us, ducking and diving, and turned up full of smiles. Ashton, for some mad reason, was carrying a handbag. And then the police arrived. Two vans, three cars, and not a horse in sight. So much for the US Bleeding Cavalry!

"Jihad!" yelled Sha. "Yippee, fucking jihad! Sack Granada! Drive out the fucking infidel!"

"Granada?" said Ash. "What – are the TV here?"

"Ash," I said. "You've got a handbag, boy. Are you trying to tell us something?"

"He's stolen it," said Gough, risking his face, in my opinion. But Ashton maybe didn't hear.

"I'm holding it for a lady-friend," he said. "Leigh-Ann, remember? Someone squashed her nose."

"Thus making her strangely better-looking and attactive," said Sha-hid. He left a beat, for comic timing. "To a randy twat like Ashton, anyway. Her face looks like a pink blancmange with raspberry sauce. I like eating white girls, but this is something else!"

The police, to be quite honest, made it worse. They were a challenge, maybe. A common enemy, for pikies and squaddies both. They poured out of their vehicles, batons drawn, riot helmets on, and waded in like men demented. And women, too, some of them half my size, and I'm no giant despite me nickname. They laid about them left and right, cracking heads and kicking legs and arses in the approved manner, and I guess they must have been using sprays as well, because lots of people fell back pretty sharpish, which isn't exactly normal in this sort of do. Then everyone regrouped and countercharged, and another shop window went in, and this one set off an alarm that boomed and brayed at a million bleeding decibels. Then two more vans turned up, from the opposite direction, with grills over their fronts, and they began to push into the crowds and some of the screaming changed into real fear, not just a jolly jamboree. I'm pretty sure I saw one girl go down under, and Sha made as if to run towards her, and Ashton held him back and shouted really loud at him.

It was getting harder and harder to stay out of it, though, if only because of the spreading of the battle. But there were whistles now, and a sort of loudspeaker booming gibberish, and some serious beating going on from clubs and batons. I saw one of the smaller police girls – no helmet, no face visor, blonde hair in a bunch under her cap – lift a stick into the air and our CSM step out of the ruck and punch her in the face and knock her over. Then he went to kick her and the ginger SAS man grabbed his upper arm and put a hold on it I think, because it stopped him dead. He turned towards Ginger, but his face was excruciated, and he didn't try to belt him or owt. The police girl got up, brave lass, and tried to stop her nose from pissing blood, but she was crying. The CSM didn't hit her any more – he couldn't – but he disappeared into the crowd damn sharp, I'm telling you.

After that, though, the end was coming soon. First off came two army trucks, like bats out of hell, but not with reinforcements – they were empty, and the backs were down already. Two sergeants in uniform jumped out and started bawling at the squaddies to get in, and they weren't looking for any funny answers, they looked fucking ugly. Ashton saw his chance and jumped for one of them, and we followed on like a bunch of rabbits. Gough and Shahid arrived at the tailgate simultaneously, and somehow Gough got tumbled to the ground, he slipped I think. Then Sha shouted: "Look out lads, the RMPs are here," and squaddies rushed up from every bleeding angle to get in. Just to put the lid on, pikey trucks had the same idea. A rattletrap collection of pick-ups and five tonners festooned with scrap and crap and children poured out of side streets and alleyways, and the gippo hardmen dived for them. Within two minutes our truck was bouncing off through the crowds and broken glass, horn blasting, people dodging every which way rather than get crushed. By one of them weird coincidences we saw Ally and Leigh-Ann right on the edge of it, and Leigh-Ann was all tears and snot, end of the world job, one shoe off and limping.

"Yo!" shouted Ashton. "Present from Santa, baby!" and sent her handbag flashing through the air. She caught it with one hand – she should of played for fucking England! – and her piggy little mush was suddenly all smiles again. Funny, females, ain't they? We looked back down the main street and the crowds were melting too, the fun was almost over. Our second truck was starting out, a cop was trying to stop the driver but wasn't having any luck, and the rest were hammering the pikies with their batons as they joined the other rubbish on their flats and pick-ups.

"Good night out," said Ashton. "Yeah, very good night out."

"Yeah," said Sha. "What a dump! What a gang of wankers. Makes you proud to be a Muslim!"

Gough's pasty face said balefully: "You shouldn't say that, Khan. You live in England. You should be proud of it."

There were at least two dozen racists in the wagon. There had to be, it was an army truck, it stands to reason. And every one of them who'd heard the mealy words just fell about.

Race relations in reverse. Sha was a hero. We got back to camp in time to have a few more pints.

Until the morning, everything was champion.

Eight

Martie's revenge took a fair time coming, but when it did it hit home good, and it was me that took the brunt of it. Maybe that was because I'd not backed them in the Perokeeto punch-up, but why I should have thought he'd let us off the hook in any case I can't imagine.

First problem in the morning was the hangover, next problem was it's Sunday. I came round slowly, and I really thought I might have died. There was no Martie in the room this time, thank fuck, and no Dave Hughes neither – he must have deposited the lance in his proper bed for once. Sha was beside me as per, and the other two were Ashton and Wasambu, which made me a racial minority for the first time in my life. As I lay there willing me eyes not to explode, Sambo got up, ebony and silent, slipped on some clothes, and buggered off. Wouldn't see him at service, neither – he had exemption. Sha said he carried his God around in a wrinkled leather bag between his legs, which was probably a joke but who was checking?

The hangover worried me a bit, because I'd never got one till I joined the army. I drank enough, God knows – my mum worked on the principle that kids only go mad about stuff that's banned or rationed, so I spent most of my school years smashed. Me and my sister used to raid her spirits too – we both got dead smart at adding water to the bottles, which is quite an art – and we learned the other trick, to lie and lie and lie. My sister was brilliant at this. I saw her cry once, real tears, when she was accused of nicking brandy, she just "could not believe you don't believe me! I'm your *daughter*! I do *not tell lies*!!"

She told me afterwards she'd been so pissed-off that mum suspected her that she almost ran away from home, "to teach the cow a lesson." She also told me that she'd nicked it. Well, of course.

But hangovers were different, they were new. Which either meant I was getting old and past it, or I was hammering it too much. I'd enjoyed the army once. For the first six months I'd almost loved it, I thought I'd found my fucking slot. Just wars. Killing mad Muslims for the good of all, including them of course. Now my eyeballs were about to burst and I wondered what the fuck. Yeah. What the fuck.

Shahid was excused services as well as Sambo, obviously – but he never missed. It was him and the only other Asian that I ever met inside, a lad called Jamal, that made me realise what a prat I'd been at first for saying no. Jamal went to services for a quiet life, the way he rode all the other punches and all the other insults from the English lads. Then he quit, with depression, and everybody laughed their tits off, which just goes to show, don't it? He's probably a terrorist by now, who knows? I would be.

Funny though. Canon Fodder (as we called the padre, ho bloody ho) couldn't persuade me, and he used every underhand trick known to men of God. First time, in the first week after intake, would you believe, he bowls into the lecture room, unannounced, and stands there looking at us like we were meant to know something. We weren't, of course: that was the technique. Every morning since we'd got to Catterick there'd be something new sprung on us, and we were meant to be confused. Sometimes weapons, sometimes the rules of combat, sometimes HIV. Then one day it's this dude in a major's uniform (that was a guess; at this time I still didn't have a clue) and a dog collar. That was the giveaway. He looks all round the room, and smiles the smile, and parks his fat arse on the table at the front.

"Good morning, men," he said. "You all believe in God, I trust? Any Moslems here? Any Jews? Any Hindus, Sikhs, or Parsis? Well, we all believe in God, don't we?" Joke coming: "Even Catholics! There's only one God, even if we give him different names!"

There was something about him that got right on my tits. Even his crack about the Catholics, which was aimed at the Scousers I imagine, didn't win me over, although I'd already had a dose or two of Scouser medicine since I joined up. I felt like saying "how d'you know He's not a She?" but I couldn't be arsed. It's a line my mum and sister used to kick about when Vronnie (that's my sister) was small enough to half believe. "I believe in God and Germaine Greer," she said once, and it brought the house down. Germaine Greer was old some Aussie dyke apparently, back in history.

He was going on, though, and I suddenly realised we were going to have a prayer. Just like that, on a Tuesday morning in a dump in Catterick. A sort of taster, before we got down to the nitty-gritty. No one had denied that they believed, no one had said "hang on, no way, fuck off." Or anything.

"We needn't kneel," he said. "It's strictly non-denominational, and we don't want to mess up your new finery. But let's close our eyes, shall we? And clasp our hands."

Shit! I couldn't do it! I didn't want to do it! I'd even raised it in the recruiting office, the religion thing, and they'd fell about and said no way! Another of their little lies.

"Sir!" I gabbled. "I'm sorry, sir – I don't, sir! I mean, I don't... I ain't got no religion, sir! Excuse me!"

"He's a conshie!" someone shouted, and the others fell about. Not Canon Fodder, though. He waited till the noise died down, and he looked as if I'd laid a toolie underneath his nose.

"Forgive me, men," he said, "if I don't join in your mirth. This... gentleman..." He stopped. Everyone was silent. "Name?" he asked me. "Rank?"

"Hassan, sir. Andrew. Um..." I didn't have a rank I knew of, and damn well he knew it too. "Er. Recruit, sir. Soldier."

"I doubt that," he said. "What platoon? What section? Who's your sergeant?"

There was a good long pause. I didn't fucking know, did I? My mind was blank.

"Please sir, I can't remember, sir," I said. They called him Big Knob, my sergeant at induction. He called *himself* Big Knob. I couldn't say that to an officer, could I? Least of all a bleeding reverend.

"Can you remember why you don't believe in God?" he said. "Or is that beyond your intellectual capacity also?"

I was blushing, I felt like shit. But if I had a passion, if my mum had brought me up with anything like that at all, it was a belief that God did not exist, or if he did he was a bastard. (Or she. Let's hear it for little Vronnie, eh?) I'm not the most best-speaking sort of person normally, I come from Blackburn, for fuck sake. But I could play the parrot sometimes, and today it came out good. My mother talking. Years and years and years.

"It's a jerrybuilt construction, sir," I said. "It's something men dreamed up because we'd be terrified to be just animals clinging to a ball of... er... rock in nothingness. It's a baby's dodie, sir. A comfort blanket. A dummy tit."

I think he'd geared himself up to be furious, but he was over-whelmed by my mates. They weren't mates at all, they were just would-be's like myself. Poor lost bastards who'd do anything for a laugh, and laugh at anything, an' all. They fell about. They howled. They went hoarse.

"He said tit, sir! He said tit! Can he say that, sir, you're a vicar, sir! He said tit! And we was praying, sir! Oooh, *sir*!"

That was him fucked, too. That was the two of us. But I realised I was fucked for good; he wasn't. And nor was Shahid, neither, who'd joined in mocking me and was a blatant liar obviously, because whatever else he was, he wan't no bleeding Christian. Later, when I got to know him (and his name), I found we had a lot in common on the God subject, and that he chose to go to church an' all that bollocks quite deliberate, like he ate proper food and not the special shite the cookhouse did for Muslims and the other "mad minori-ties." Not like poor Jamal. They wrecked him in nine weeks.

When the shouting had died down, Canon F had got it all worked out again. The crazy bastard didn't dismiss me, he suggested that everyone should pray *for* me, to "help me to enlightenment." That got to me I must say, although I tried my hardest not to let it, and it got to the others as well, because there probably wasn't one believer in the whole damn lot of them. They was screwed as well, see, and they couldn't slide out now, could they? They were *officially* believers, ganged up against the lousy heathen – me! So every church parade from here to Kingdom Come had got them on the list, and the padre could tick all the boxes when the questionnaires came round. Atheists? We don't have them – our men believe. Like the army don't have racists, and the army don't have bullies, and the army don't have crackheads, and the army don't have gays. Like fuck they don't. Like fuck.

At the end of it, I couldn't get a punishment, because you can't be forced to believe can you, even in the army? Major Fodder just told me that he'd suggest certain duties for me every Sunday, nice and early, in lieu of sitting in the chapel with my friends. I wouldn't want to waste my time, would I? And I could have no objection he could see, no way. I got sent to the kitchens usually, to pick my nose and fart off Saturday night's vindaloo and lager, and like most army punishments it was completely pointless, and more or less forgotten in three weeks. Except that my "non-believer status" was on my file, and everyone always knew, and every time we went on an exercise or to a different camp or anything, I had to tell, and explain, and hang about like a spare prick, and it was mega, mega boring.

Shahid used to take the piss as well. He said what if we were wrong and there *was* a God or Allah in the clouds? He'd get seventy three virgins – Muslim perks – and I'd get eternal hell. Actually he said it was a mistranslation and he'd only get a bunch of grapes, and he'd have to kill a Christian anyway to make it as a martyr, which might get him into trouble with the padre. So in the end, sometimes, I went to services just for the crack, and to stop them asking stupid questions. Part-time believer, sort of. Look good on a job CV that would, eh?

Anyway, this Sunday morning – the day of Mart's revenge – religion turned out to be the least of my worries. The padre down here was a boring bastard, I'd found out the week before, but today the Lord had other plans for me. I had a shower and a shit to clear the stale booze out, but as Sha and Ash and me went to the eatery we clocked alien activity. Outside the main block was two police cars, and there was a lot of lads milling about, and a lot of officers. This caused a buzz for us. Maybe some pikie had got killed! When we queued up for our scran, though, we heard it was much worse. They'd let the coppers into camp because they'd had to; they'd got a warrant or some fucking thing. It was a tin-lid job apparently. The town was well pissed off with constant trouble from the squaddies, and heads were going to roll. Someone, at long long last, was going to be in the shit. Up to the testicles.

Chas Hicks and Bollocks Bowyer were jumping up and down like blue-arsed flies.

"It's bloody typical," Chas was screeching. "We sort their gippoes out for 'em and all we get is blame. Jesus, they've been nicking stuff and raping girls for yonks and the fuzz have done fuck all. They don't know they're born, these sheep-shaggers!"

"Gratitude!" said Bollocks. "That's what they ought to give us, they ought to give us fucking medals! They're trying to arrest blokes! Squaddies! I'll tell you what, we'll break the place up tonight, no danger! Last night'll be like a poofters' pantie party!"

I had a sudden picture of the cop-girl and the CSM. It was a real punch. It could have smashed her face in.

"Bastard coppers," said a lad I didn't know. "I got one a good kick up the arse, I know that much. They've got no bloody right!"

"They'll not do much," said Shahid, soothingly. "We're fireproof in here, it's strictly invitation only, the police have got no jurisdiction."

"You what? Talk English can't you, Stanley!"

"We don't even have to let them in," said Shahid. "That plain enough for you, Dumbo?"

"Fucking Paki," said Bollocks, in disgust. "They've took Martie in, in any case. That serious enough for you, is it?"

Ashton snorted.

"So who's that up there, then? Bloody Elton John?"

That shut Bowyer up, because Martie was walking through the door right then, followed by Big Dave and Billy 'Unt. It shut me up, too, because the lance stalked straight up to me with a sort of hardman sneering look. I noticed his mug was even worse than the day before – bent nose, black eye, and now a good split lip. Couldn't fail to notice really, because he stuck his face right up to mine and he wasn't going to kiss me, neither.

"You!" he said. "Get in that office! Now! Where's your mate?"

I goggled. If I had mates they were there in front of him.

"What for?" I said. "What mate?"

"The other yellow bastard. The other pansy toerag. Gough."

Ashton fell about.

"They've found you out, Ti! Goughie's your bestest pal!"

"Shut the fuck up, you!" snapped Martie. "Where is he, Hassan? The captain wants you in the office. He's bloody livid! Now!"

"What for?" I said again. "I mean..."

"Are you refusing, soldier? *Shift!*"

It was madness. It was upsetting, if you know what I mean. But five minutes later I was standing in front of Captain Sanders listening to what I'd done. It was terrible, I was a thug, a ringleader, and it was only because my lancejack had stood up for me that he'd persuaded the police not to "pursue the matter." What matter? He wouldn't tell me. I couldn't ask. I fucking *knew*!

He was a tall man, this Captain, probably not thirty, with rimless specs. After his little bit of shouting, he played the kindly uncle bit, only disapproving. More in sorrow than in anger, that sort of diarrhoea.

"But I didn't do it, sir," I said. "That's the honest truth, sir. I didn't do nothing. Anything."

The look of sorrow got more sorrowful.

"Hassan," he said. "Can't you just tell the truth for once? Can't you be man enough?" He sighed. "Not in your nature, I suppose. Something you just can't bring yourself to do. Ah well."

He'd been standing up, now he sat down. He picked up a pen and marked something on the pad in front of him. He was going slightly bald.

"So now you're insulting your own lance corporal," he said. "Now you're calling him a liar. I'm sending you back to Catterick. You and Private Gough. We can do without you here. The pair of you."

What to say to that? Some fucking punishment, I *don't* think!

"Yes, sir. Sorry, sir."

I knew the rules, the regs, and so did he. I could do no right, and he could do no wrong. If he moved, salute him. If he spoke, apologise. I wondered vaguely where Gough had got to. Perhaps he'd done a runner. Perhaps he wasn't as stupid as he looked.

Late that afternoon, they put me on a train and sent me back to Yorkshire, which some would say was punishment enough. Out of all the bastards in the ruck last night, me and Goughie were the only ones to get it in the neck. He hadn't done a runner, by the way, he'd been having a crap. I didn't see him on the train, cause he avoided me, and it didn't take much working out that he blamed me for everything, including grassing him up (and myself as well, presumably, the stupid twat.)

I did have a conversation with the ginger SAS man, though, who turned out to be a pretty decent bloke, and it passed the time away. He laughed like a drain when I said we'd thought he was something undercover, but he did ask me about my mates in the army, about Sha and Ashton, and if it had turned out as good as I'd hoped it would when I joined up. I didn't want to go on too much, in case I bored the tits off him, but I did tell him how they'd conned me out of learning a trade, which was why I'd come in in the first place. He said my timing was unlucky. The only skill they really needed in a squaddie nowadays was to keep the numbers up – and stop a bullet, naturally.

I found out later that he'd had a talk to Gough as well, in another carriage. From what I gathered, Gough had told him Shahid was a terrorist, some sort of Muslim nutter. And Ashton was a maniac for sex.

You've got to laugh, ain't you? That Goughie. What a bleeding dick.

Crap-Hats to the Slaughter

One

I'd not had much to do with Sergeant Williams before I got sent back to Catterick, except working out how to avoid him. He was on intake mainly – because he was too brainless to do a proper job, was the general feeling when you got to know him. Pretty bog standard of the army to think that new recruits weren't important, but it wasn't like that, exactly. Some of the new lads took to him big style, because he was hard and macho and everything that lots of kids had joined for, I guess – so that they could be like him. He was a mate of Martie Martin ditto. Which said it all for me.

I was eating on me own on the first morning of my "punishment," half through choice, when I clocked him coming to my table. He smiled the smile, which gave me fair warning there was shit to follow, and reached across and picked a sausage off my plate.

"Worth eating are they? Or just the usual shite?"

Why wait for my opinion? He held it between his thumb and finger and sniffed at it hard, snot rattling in his throat. Then he give it a lick, all up its length like a prick in a porno, and smacked his lips. Then he dropped it back on my plate, right in the middle of the fried egg that I was eating.

"Yerk," he said. "Fucking vile. I don't know why you put up with it. Shoot the cook, I say. Where's your mate? Your bumboy? Gough?"

How should I know? I hadn't really seen that stubborn bastard since we'd got out of the taxi from the station. The ginger SAS man had taken it, and let us share for free an' all, which was amazing, unbelievable. But there were only seven soldiers on our whole floor when we got back to our lines, and Goughie even moved his stuff to the furthest empty room that he could find away from me, to make it clear that we weren't mates. (He must've thought I didn't know!) We weren't even talking, it turned out, even in the taxi. We were like a married couple waiting for the kids to die so we could get divorced.

Anyway, to cut a long story short, Williams had decided humiliation would be the best thing for my soul, the smartest punishment, so I was going to be his "bitch" to help him with the latest intake, who'd come in the night before. Williams, who was white (or Liverpudlian at least), fancied he could do the 'ard-man Yardie talk (he couldn't) and even did it with the 'ard-man black recruits we got sometimes. They had to take it, naturally, not because he was hard himself (he was) but because he was a sergeant. Ashton had been one of the few black lads who'd took the piss once, months ago. He never did again. My role, my part in it, would be to show the poor new trogs about, take them to where Williams told me to take them, answer their stupid moron questions, wipe their arses if they needed it.

"You're trained, see," he said. "The government have put a lot of cash in you, and we've got to make some use of it, ain't we? You can strip down an SA80, can't you, la'? And fire the fucking thing, although I doubt if you can hit a target. And you can drive a War-rior, and service it, and work a radio, and march an 'undred mile in full kit with a cooker and a kitchen sink stuffed up yer arse and turn water into wine if you're stranded in the desert. Can't yer?"

Oh aye, I thought. And sleep suspended by me foreskin up Mount Everest, and boil a kettle with a candle in an Arctic gale, and shit standing on me fucking head. And within six months or so I was off to Helmand or Sangin to show the madmen of the world we were the sane ones, and they should vote like us, and have an English God, and never drink and drive, not even on a camel. I could even tell them why, if anyone was dumb enough to ask. Cause the Yankees say so, right? Don't you for-bleeding-get it.

"Well?" said Williams. "Are you dumb as well as fucking stupid? All that training needs some use, don't it? And why you dressed up like a plumber on a call? You're on punishment, have you forgot? I'll give you thirty seconds to go and get your combats on. And don't forget to clean your plate away. Whoops. Butterfingers!"

As I went to stand – I didn't bother to say I'd been told the night before to put on coveralls – he tipped my plate up and shot the leftovers across the plastic tabletop. I saw some squaddies smile and snigger but I just got a pile of paper and pushed it all back on again. He watched me set off for the bin.

"Outside here in five mins, Hassan. Don't keep me fucking waiting. Twenty press-ups for every second that you're late."

It was the second day for the new intake of crap-hats, and as we went across towards the big reception hall, they did look pretty comical, I must say. They all tried marching everywhere, because they thought that's what they had to do, and unlike on the first day, the corporals and the sergeants had dropped their Mr Nice Guy act. As we came round the corner one NCO was screaming: "Don't fucking march, you fucking twats! You can't even fucking walk yet! You look like a crowd of pregnant chimpanzees!"

"Cunts," said Sergeant Williams, affably. "Where *do* we dredge 'em up from? Look at the hair on that one. Look at that kid's keks. Has he shit 'em, do you reckon?"

The faces were amazing. Pale and pasty most of them, mostly scrawny, some with puppy fat. About fifty came past us, sort of marching, sort of stumbling, and only two of them looked two points above completely useless. Which the sergeant seemed to think was a good thing.

"We had another Scotch lot in yesterday," he said. "Train down from Glasgow, coach from Darlington. They're mad them Scotchies, do you know that? All pissed. Every last man jack of 'em. Man *Jock*, I mean, geddit? The bus was full of sick. Diced carrots and tomato skins. The stink was 'angin'. Animals."

"Good fighters, though," I said. I couldn't call it racist because it was true, the Scots who joined when I did were completely mad. They did lines of coke before going to the gym in the morning. They drank Scotch and lager even in the church. And they fought. Each other. Us. Pub landlords, punters, coppers in the street. All the regiments, all the lads from different parts of England, were trained to get at each other, it was meant to keep us on our toes, to make us proud. But the Jocks were different. They *really* hated us. It was mutual.

"Aye. 'Cause they're brought up wearing skirts maybe. They put up with a lot of stick. Or maybe it's cold breezes on their bollocks. Anyway, enough chit-chat, la'. You've got work to do."

The next few hours, in the big reception room, were really jack, really mega-boring, and stank of sweat and farts. The lads were all crammed in, but it was pretty quiet, because no one had a lot to say, they'd only met each other the day before and they were nervous. A normal life chucked up, four years to go unless you dared to take the instant get-out clause (and the taunts and insults if you did), and nothing to ease the growing feeling of disaster but smoking and self-pity. Shit city, except you couldn't shit 'cause no one can, the first few days. Hence the smell of botty-gas.

First off, the poor saps were sorted into their regiments, which involved queuing up for endless ages while junior officers and senior NCOs clucked and fannied round with piles of paperwork, and told them lies about why they'd be better off in such-and-such a mob and not the one they thought that they were joining. It wasn't the only lie they'd heard before they got here, you bet your life on it. At the recruiting offices where I joined, they sort of talked the pay up sky-high as well, and failed to mention what came out of it, just little things like food and rent, and life-insurance. Can you imagine it? They charge you for your scoff, which any self-respecting pig would turn its nose up at, and they charge you for your sty, which ditto, and they charge you in case you lose a leg or bollock "fighting for your country!" The only cash I heard a mention of was the special bonus if I joined up fast, and joined the infantry. They didn't tell me why, though. They didn't mention the big black holes they'd buried all the money in. And the infantry.

My job today, my punishment, was to wander in among the new lads with the sergeant, and smile, and wink, and give the proper answers to any awkward questions they might ask. It was a bit like when I did exams at uni in a way, except the smell of farts was stronger. I looked at all these faces, the hard, the scared, the dopey, and it was more a blur than anything. Mostly the things they asked were stupid – like "are we allowed to smoke?" and "how long do we get to have our dinner" – but sliding to the ridiculous, like "is it good here, will I like it, do you reckon?" I could mumble something stupid back, and I could lie in my teeth about how smart it was, but I couldn't engage my brain in it, no way, and every now and then Williams would rip the piss off me to entertain them, and I'd put on a smile and they'd have a nervous laugh.

"He don't mind, lads," said Williams. "He's a big soft twat is Tiny. Any Scousers here? Any 'ardmen from da good old 'Pool? Aye, I can see it in your eyes, nice one la'! Well, 'e's from Lancashire, int'e, a fucking woollyback. Worse, from bleeding Blackburn, need I say more? Just laugh away!"

Every now and then he got his knife in someone, too, and made it plain he'd "marked their card for them." A pale-faced blond one in particular, his hair so light you could see his pink skull through it. The sergeant really picked on him.

"Look at that," he said to me. "Over there, by that window. He's like a pink-eyed fucking fairy. What the fuck's he wearing, tell me tha'?"

A dead good jacket is what. Brilliant. That's what Sergeant Williams meant, I guess – he fancied it. He moved in sharpish, and I had to follow. To spread a little peace and joy. He touched the lad on the shoulder from behind, and he jumped half out of his skin.

"Hiya la'," he said. "Boss jacket, eh? Look even better on a man, know worra mean?"

The lad was tall like Sergeant Williams, but not so stocky. Probably ten years younger though, and not a sergeant. Not anything. A trog. A crap-hat. His pale face went bright scarlet in half a second, it seemed to glow. He tried a smile, but he was smart enough to realise he'd done something wrong. Like exist, for instance.

"Yeah," he said. "Er... sir. I got it at the weekend."

This could have been the cue for Williams to get nasty. You were told not to call NCOs sir even before they got you off the bus. Officers were sir, no bugger else. You could get hanged for calling a sergeant sir. Castrated with a rusty spoon. But the sergeant just smiled a great big sunny smile.

"Good choice, Al – it's fucking A. I'm going to buy it off of you."

The lad's eyes were pale an' all, and you could read them like a book. They said "You what!? Sod off, why don't you!" But his mouth said, "Er. Um. I'm not really with you, sir. It's not for sale."

He was swallowing, and his Adams apple bobbed up in his neck like a giraffe. Long neck. Big Adams apple. Williams's smile went harder. The other crap-hats were watching now. Mouse and snake. Breakfast.

"Don't call me sir, la'. I'll have to Agai you, know what that is, do you? Agai 67. I said I like your coat. I'll give you forty quid for it."

The eyelids were blinking now. The eyes were looking hunted.

"But. But I only got it at the weekend...er..."

"Sergeant," I said. And the sergeant glared at me. First warning.

"Sergeant," said the crap-hat gratefully. "I mean... I mean it cost me eighty pounds. Um, eighty five. My mother bought—"

Bad mistake. All the other trogs were laughing. Oh the release! Release of pressure. Not for the victim, though.

"Ah," said Sergeant Williams. "Ain't that nice? Did I say forty, Al? Make that thirty five. No, make it thirty. Bloody hell la', you drive a hard bargain. But thass my last offer, you tight cunt. I ain't goin' any lower."

The trog's eyes went from him to me, as if there was something *I* could do about it. The sergeant's eyes went on me too, and the last traces of a smile had gone. He fished his wallet out. Honest to God, he had a wallet, that's how bleeding low he was.

"Don't fuck me about, son," said Williams. "It'll be twenty five if you make me wait much longer. Last offer, take it or leave it."

"Leave it? Can I—"

"No you fucking can't, you dildo. Count of three. Going, going—"
He jerked three notes out, and snapped them between his thumb
and fingernails. The crap-hat was brighter than a beetroot.

"Gone," said Williams, almost conversational. "Now get the bastard
off before I kill you. Tiny here'll tell you. I will, won't I, Tiny? I
fucking will."

My eyes locked with the poor sod's, but only for an instant. Then
he was looking downwards, and the jacket was half off. Oh fuck, I
thought, just what the fuck is this? Just what the fuck is going on? I
felt his eyes go on me again and I couldn't look at all, I felt like utter
shit.

The sergeant took the jacket and looked at it with contempt, as if it
was a disappointment, utter crap.

"You see," he said. "That didn't hurt much, did it, la'? It didn't
hurt at all. Sergeant Williams," he added. "In case you might
forget. Not sir, but *Sergeant* Williams. And this here's Tiny, me latest
bitch, know wharra mean? He does everything for me. And I mean
*every*thing."

He threw the jacket at me.

"Carry that," he said. "You can take it down to Oxfam later, maybe.
Jesus, I'm so generous it's embarrassing. Walk on, bitch. We got
more work to do."

I saw the pale boy later in the day, when all the formal stuff was finished, and we were going to the Naafi bar. When I say we, I mean the squaddies, not recruits, they aren't allowed to drink for the first six weeks, they aren't allowed inside a licensed place at all, on or off the camp. They aren't allowed off the camp either, come to that, so no chance of getting plastered anyway. No drink, no drugs, no sex except for Mrs Palm, no mobile in your pocket to call your mum or girlfriend if you needed a good cry. People did get stuff of course, especially the drugs, which you could hide much easier than a vodka bottle. Mobiles were pretty easy, too, but they were frowned on big style. If one went off in a lecture room, or on the range, it was shit up to your trollybobs.

No, I saw the lad when I was going to the bar, and on my own, thank Christ. Apart from me and Goughie, the five on our floor who weren't down south were the usual bag of walking wounded, with the three youngest bunged up to the eyeballs with depression pills. It's the quickest way these days if you miss the "get out of jail free" slots – you get depressed and with luck you get discharged. Not so long ago, they reckon, most of it was sham, but now it's real. With half the army suicidal, the brass fight back by keeping you in until your head actually explodes. Which means that Catterick's chockful of nutcases in uniform – who merge in nicely with the local population! The other two were older men, sane or mad I wouldn't like to say. They seemed to hate each other in their own right, and every other bastard for good measure. The one I'd spoke to came from Cheshire, where posh people live, the polite society. He was carrying a rubber ring.

"Charlie Spencer." He didn't stick his hand out or nothing; so much for polite society. "Just back from Germany. Operation for me bastard piles. What you here for?"

Why lie? Too much like hard work.

"We had a riot. Down on the exercise. I got kicked back. Punishment."

"Lucky bastard. Cushy, eh? How long you been in?"

"Oh, about eight month. I dunno."

"Eh! Eight month! Cushy! 'Ere – see that locker there? Name on it says Khan. Is that a fucking Paki name?"

Why argue? Too much like hard work.

"Well, he's an Asian, like. He's alright, he comes from Oldham."

His eye turned nasty. It was as if I'd said a sewage farm.

"Oldham! It's fucking full of 'em, that is! Dump! Nice lad my arse." He paused. "Any more in, is there? I hate Pakis, me. I always said, the day they let a Paki in, the British Army's dead! I'll shoot him if I see the bastard, straight up I will. It's mine, okay? It's fucking *ours*! When's he coming back? I tell you, I can't hardly wait!"

Sane, then. Barking sane. That was that one solved.

101

As I approached the Naafi, I saw more trouble fronting up for me, and I was getting sick of it, quite honestly, well sick. The pale trog was waiting for me, and he was with a bunch of other crap-hats. I tensed. Maybe they were going to fill me in. Oh, not another bleeding fight. I was really, really sick of it.

"Hi, lad," I said. "Sorry about all that shit earlier. You'll get to know Sarnt Williams. He's a cunt."

His eyes opened in a sort of shock. Unexpected, that. Jesus, it even surprised me, the way I said it. Well 'ard; not.

"Oh," he said. "Oh. Bloody hell, like. Thanks."

Well, don't get too excited, I thought, it don't mean I'm your best mate. I don't give a shit for you, tell the honest truth.

"Yeah," I said. "Well, see you, then. I've got to get a drink. I'm gaggin'"

They were all looking at me, curiously. Like in a zoo. I was in combats. Sergeant's orders. I'd be in combats till I hit the pit. Day after bleeding day.

He said: "But it's... it's sort of stealing, isn't it? Is he allowed to do that? I mean, I said it weren't for sale."

"You took money for it, Jeff," said one of them. Jeff. I'd really thought his name was Al. Albino. It hit me. Jesus. That bloody Williams.

"I know," said the boy, unhappily. "Christ, what's my mother going to bloody say?"

Nobody laughed this time.

"Can I complain?" he said. "I mean – is there someone I can talk to?"

I didn't have to think for long. But I was trying to be kind.

"Not really, mate. I mean, you can, but it'd be quicker just to cut your own throat, save them the trouble."

"Shit, that's really tight," said someone. "You can't be serious?"

He sounded just like my sister Vronnie. But I made a face, then smiled.

"Who'd believe you, mate?" I said. "He's a sergeant, ain't he? They'd tell you to go and fuck yourself."

"But I've got witnesses! *You* saw it, didn't you? You were there! What are you, are you a corporal or something?"

"I'm a squaddie, and I need a fucking drink," I said. "Get real, okay? You're in the fucking army. I'm not a corporal and I never fucking will be. If I said Williams had robbed you of that coat I'd be a corpse. You sold it to him. Get real."

They stood around and watched me go in silence. Food for fucking thought, I thought – surely some stupid bastard knows the rules of joining up? For the first six weeks you can just walk away, you've got the right, never mind what some bastard sergeant tells you. So do it. Do it while you can. Just do it.

'Cause one day soon you'll find it is too late, my friends. You'll find out soon you've missed the bleeding boat.

And then there's four more years until the next one sails… By then you could be dead and bloody buried.

Two

I tried to have a wank that night, to take my mind off everything. I was in a room all on my own, which was one good thing when the lines were empty, and I tried to conjure Bridgie up. It's hard to get a proper hard-on for a girl when you don't like her any more though, especially if you think she never liked you anyway. She'd even stopped texting now, more or less. It was safe to leave my mobile on again, not that I bothered much. I got one sometimes out of the blue, usually insulting and unpleasant, usually about money. The cheeky cow said I'd knocked off her CDs and her iPod, which is bollocks. Whatever she'd had for two whole years, she'd had off me.

I realised after a while the end was soft and useless, and I worried that I'd still gone on, absent-minded, like. Bloody hell, that was like a little kid does, isn't it – pressing and prodding it for comfort, like twiddling your hair. I didn't want to stop though, in case it meant I'd lost interest in sex, so I tried to think of someone else. I hit on Emma then, a girl I'd met at college as I was leaving to go to uni and she was signing on. She was young and blonde and pretty lively and I got it off another girl she fancied me. Big deal – I didn't see her for ages after that, till I met her on the station one Saturday afternoon. I was in combats, and we had a jokey conversation, she was very flirty, and called me General, which she thought was pretty smart. Afterwards, two or three times, we met again, and she told me once, while she was pissed, that I could have her if I wore me uniform! She didn't mean it though. I tried to bring her up into my mind, and stripped her jeans off, and her knickers and her top. Her tits were Bridgie's though – quite small, with big spready nipples. This wasn't going to work at all.

Quite lucky really, because when I'd given up, the bloody door banged open and a pissed-up bloke barged in. He turned the light on and blinded me, then he let out a rousing fart. It was the other old guy, the one who wasn't Charlie Spencer, and he didn't seem to really know where he was.

"Hey!" I went. "Oi, mate. What you doing? I'm in my fucking pit."

It wasn't very late, so I suppose he had a right to be confused. He stood there blinking for a good long time, and he hadn't really focused on me yet. He was a big bloke, but he wasn't tall, and his belly looked too fat for him to be a soldier – he wasn't fit, he couldn't be. To me – no judge – he looked fifty if a day. Could he be, and still be in the army? Still be just a squaddie, come to that?

He cleared his throat. His voice was deep and Yorkshire, Huddersfield, Leeds, somewhere over that way. It wasn't the slightest bit unfriendly.

"You're in *my* fucking pit, you mean," he said. "What is this, a present from the Captain, or am I seeing things? I've had this room a week now. I've not seen you before, have I?"

He had seen me, although we hadn't spoke. And I had slept in this bed the night before, and on me own.

"I've spoke to your oppo," I said. "Yesterday. Charlie Spencer."

"That twat. Well any mate of Charlie's an enemy of mine, so I'm sorry, lad, you're less than bleeding welcome. To my room, my bed, my body, fucking anything. Either you go or I do. What's it to be?"

This was getting serious, it *was* my bed. I'd slept in it, this bloke was drunk or mad or both. Now, to put the tin lid on, he sat down on the end, he plonked himself, and even with the army lack of springs he bounced me in the air.

"I'm called Ken," he said. "I like you, son. Shall we have a drink? I've got a bottle in me cupboard, it's called a locker but it doesn't lock. I've got some brandy and me old guitar."

He was up again, and I was bouncing, and he wrenched the locker door and it came open. Empty, naturally.

"Fuck, I've been burgled! Fucking fucking fuck, that were *drei Stern*, German three star! And the guitar were a Martin, fuck my boots!"

I doubted that, but then you never know, do you? I'd've liked a Martin but I'd never had the chance. I'd've liked to have my guitar with me, even, it was a sort of comfort, but I'd been warned in no uncertain terms. Squaddies don't like proper music, and they don't like people doing things they can't, and most of all they can't stand folk, the crap my mother brought me up on. If you wanted to get beat up, you might as well just try Morris dancing, go the whole damn hog! If this bloke really had a Martin they'd have smashed it, was my feeling. Destroyed it. Either that or he must be awful, awful hard.

Suddenly, he crashed out of my room without another word, and I thought bugger it, he's left the bleeding light turned on. No hurry though, I was well awake by now, I might even get up again and toddle off and get another lager, sure as shit I'd not see him again. Funny if he did have a Martin, though, he did look like a folkie in a way – fat gut and alcoholic. It made me miss the sorts of dumps I'd spent half my life in, despite the fact my mates all thought that I was mad. Not just the music, neither. The whole damn bit.

He did have a Martin though, and he had a bottle ditto – next door down the passage where his room really was. He came back in laughing, guitar in one hand, brandy in the other, flipped the bottle on my bed, nodded, winked, and struck a chord. Then started cranking up his B-string with his tongue between his teeth.

"Pissed!" he said. "Hang on. That sound better? That's it. Get some glasses, can't you? I've done my fucking bit."

I was a bit self-conscious standing up in only a little teeshirt but what the hell? Bridgie had failed me so there was no embarrassment there, and the three star brandy looked just the job. I found a cup, and gave him the water glass, and while I poured he played a pattern of chords that sounded great.

"Is it a Martin then?" I said. "Honest to God?"

"Is it fuck as like! Got nicked years ago, that did. Johnny Roadhouse cheapo, I buy a new one every time some drunk cunt buggers it. What you want? English, Irish, Scottish, bluegrass, Dylan, blues, Bert Jansch, Bogle, or some other modern shite? I don't do rock and pop though, mate. I'm too old and it's too crappy. Gimme that brandy. Cheers!"

The session started then, and just went on and on. He was amazing, this drunk old get, he had a voice like nails – not like his speaking voice – and he played brilliant. Every now and then he stopped to suck down three star, and give me snatches from his life. He'd come back from Krautland with Charlie Spencer for "a medical complaint" but he didn't say what it was, and he drank the brandy in big gulps, never letting up. It was a litre bottle, and he was pissed before we started, and although I kept my end up I was outclassed. Good stuff though – as rough as arseholes, a German supermarket's worst. And however much he supped, he never played a wrong note or muffed a chord. By the time he pushed the box at me and told me it was my turn to torture it, I was incapable. I strummed a bit, I bolloxed up my chords and words, and Ken laughed his cock off and chain-smoked.

And then he changed. It was gradual at first, then he went down pretty fast. He asked me if I'd ever killed a man, and I said I hadn't, and said I wasn't sure I ever could. Then I said: "It's funny that."

He looked at me across the nasty little smoky room. His eyes had sunk into his face, sort of. And he was sucking on his fag, his mouth covered by his whole hand, cupped in front of it.

"Funny?" he said. "Why? Why d'you think that's funny?"

I didn't like his tone at all. His eyes were hooded. His head was lost in smoke. I tried a smile, but I was struggling.

"Well, I dunno," I said. "I mean…well it's what I'm paid for, in't it? I guess they'd chuck me out."

"You're not paid to kill, you're paid to fucking die," he said. "Ain't you worked that out yet, you little twat?"

He was looking at the lino on the floor. He dropped his fag butt and watched it smouldering.

"Killing's all right, mate," he said. "Don't knock it till you've fucking tried." He put his foot on the dog-end and ground it out. "First time I got the chance was Kosovo. I got this bloke square in my sights and the adrenaline shot through me like a fucking fire, I went bloody near delirious. And then an officer moved in front of me. Deliberate. He could see the state that I was in. To shoot the target I'd've had to shoot him first. I bloody nearly did. I wanted to. I hated him. I fucking *hated* him."

And suddenly he picked his glass up just like that and drained it. Then he picked the brandy up, the drop left in the bottle, then his guitar. It was as if he hated me as well. His face had gone like poison. He hated me.

He nearly knocked the door frame out in leaving, and the impact of his shoulder shook the room. I could hear him in the passageway, crashing from side to side. No guitar sounds, though. He never banged it once. He didn't drop the bottle, neither.

It was well gone two o'clock. Work in the morning. I switched off the light and lay there in the bed and felt like death. I'd seen Ken's face as he'd gone out the room, and I didn't know what to make of it. It had gone from poisonous to utter fucking misery. He looked like a poor old useless sod.

Ah well, I thought. It had helped to pass the time away…

Three

Normally in camp, I'd start trying to wake up about half six, and out of bed by quarter to for block jobs. Today though, no reason to get up, I thought I'd take a little lie-in. Fat chance. Sergeant Williams didn't get to be a sergeant by being lax, and he'd decided to start his morning fun by beasting the new recruits at the crack of dawn. I was still his bitch.

He came into my room like a bloody tank at six o'clock or so, in full combats and full of piss and vinegar. He snapped the light on, and as I lay there blinking he pulled the covers off and started yelling, his idea of humour.

"Jesus, Tiny! I can see where you got your name, la'! Is that a lazy lob or have you had a hysterectomy?"

That's what he said, straight up. Even half unconscious and hungover I marvelled at his grasp of gynaecology, or at least his English. It didn't make me smile though.

"Come on!" he went. "Out, out, out! Hands off cocks, on socks, there's work to do! Sleep on your own again did you, sad bastard? Jesus, what a stink of booze and old fags! Are you a secret drinker, or was it company?"

Someone started banging on the wall then, yelling for silence, and it must have clicked with him.

"Fucking hell!" he said. "Old Ken Rogers was it? Serenade by moonlight? You want to watch it, la', he's broken lots of fucking hearts. More hearts than you've had hot fucking dinners!"

He'll break the wall down if he goes on like this, never mind hearts, I thought. If it was Ken he was in a right old rage, but his shouts and swears were muffled, like he had his head jammed in a pillow.

"Shut it, Ken, or you're on a charge!" Williams roared back at him, but he didn't seem too bothered, really.

"He's a good bloke, Ken," he told me. "Likes his brandy though, which explains the bleeding pong. He don't normally talk to twats like you, but he's off his trike now, did it show? He's been every-where, Balkans, Iraq, the 'Stan, and ended up in Deutschland cause they don't count as an enemy no more. If even that wa' too much for the poor bastard, well fuck. It's an 'oliday camp, innit?"

I wasn't really listening, but I'd picked up on the broken hearts, if nothing else.

"What you on about, Sarge?" I said. "You saying he's gay?"

He looked at me as if I'd gone insane.

"Gay? Ken Rogers? Where the fuck d'you get that from? We don't have poofs in the army, mate, ain't no one told you yet, and they weren't even invented when Ken joined up. Nah, Ken fucks women. Lots of 'em. Piles of 'em. His last wife buggered off three months ago. He went mad in Germany. Got banged up. He tried to kill the bastard that was fucking her."

"What, some Kraut?"

"Fuck no! Even Maureen wouldn't sink that low! Nah, sergeant in the Fusiliers. Famous for it. He's got four kids round here, all with different women, all faithful army wives. Got Ken down apparently. It really got to him."

I was out of bed now, three quarters dressed. My combats weren't that smart, I hadn't really bothered much the night before, but I hoped Williams would be too wrapped up in his chat to notice.

"Yeah, well I spose it would," I mumbled. "He never mentioned it, last night, though. He just sung, mainly. Sung and played. Brilliant."

"Load of folkie shite," said the sergeant. "He wouldn't know good music if you paid him. Good soldier, though. He's killed more blokes than anyone I know. Dozens of 'em, he's got nerves of steel. Well, except he's started getting weird about it, which is why they sent him off to Krautland in the first place, according to Charlie Spencer." He laughed. "Pain in the arse, really – he'll be liking Moslems next! Siding with Osama in Helmand!" He laughed again, another shout. "Pain in the arse like Charlie! D'you get it? He's got piles! Pain in the fucking arse! Now fucking hurry up. The new boys need their bleeding breakfast."

When you're in training, breakfast is the first meal that you drop, for two good reasons. One, it's followed by **PT**, which does your stomach in, and two, because it's crap. The rumour is they fry the eggs and sossies and the bacon up before they go out on the piss at knock-off, and leave them soaking in the oil overnight. What we don't eat (which is nearly all of it) they sell on to the local farms to give the pigs a treat.

But the very new boys, crap-hats, trogs – well they go to breakfast every day, and the kitchens put a special effort on for a week or two. Sometimes the egg whites are even chewable, sometimes the yolks are only hard, not concrete. Sadly that don't last, nor does the crap-hats' interest – and the more left over, the more cash-back from the farmer or the nearest prison. That's a rumour. I lost two stone in my first three months. That's a fact.

So job one today, was to wander through the ranks, Sarnt Williams on one side, me on the other, and ask them how the scoff was, and how they were, and tell them how lucky they were they wouldn't have PT today, the idle buggers. Lots of them were still smiling – on Day Three! – and some of them were probably realising that life without a hangover wasn't necessarily the end of the world. My own eyes were closed up and glued with crap, and my mouth tasted like a nun's gusset after a shag-in at the Vatican, so maybe it was a point of view. I talked the talk, but I was dreaming of a shower, nothing else.

Later, it was a case of playing escort as they traipsed from place to place, with the sergeant using me as his whipping post to show how hard he was "but fair," the twat. The idea was I'd been a naughty boy, and this is what I got for it. If any of them had had a brain at all they'd've seen that he was just a bully and a fool, and in fact I spent a lot of time making faces behind his back, eye-rolling and so on, to make the point. It occurred to me that if I tried I might get some of them to quit maybe, to go back to their mothers like they was entitled to. By fuck, that would be a stunt to work on Williams! That'd show the bastard.

The first few days are pretty weird when you join up, I could see it much more clearer now I was helping these poor sods. They'd been sorted into their lines, they'd been tipped into their companies, they'd collected their bedding and been shown a few times how to make their bed. These were the days the corporals came into their own, no answers back, right little Hitlers, and they enjoyed it. If you were lucky you got one who would show you things and didn't take the piss, but mostly you got blokes who liked to make you look a total wally. The main way to do that was to say that your company was the only ones that ever did it right, and if you didn't get your arsehole into gear you'd end up in C Coy, the biggest pile of shit in history. Or D Coy, or A Coy, it didn't matter – any Coy except the one you'd been ended up in, they were all the bleeding same in actual fact.

They also, all the NCOs right up to sergeant major, trained you up to hate somebody else. It wasn't personal, you just had to realise you was best and all the other bastards were inferiors – especially the Jocks. They were easy targets because they were like the Scousers in a way – there was something wrong with them. They always turned up drunk at every new intake, they snorted coke, and they attacked anyone and everyone, including each other, for no reason at all. Their drugs problem was mega. Massive.

Some corporals used to make us chant against the Jocks. They'd get us into groups when no officers were about and sing sort of football choruses about what poofs they were, and how they all wore skirts. In fact, in our division, anyone was a target who wasn't from the North of England, and that included Liverpudlians. The best thing we could think to say about the Scousers was that when they nicked the tracks off of the tanks it stopped us training.

As for blacks and Paks and gays, of course – hardly worth mentioning, is it? In all my training time I only knew one camp lad, one lad who actually *looked* camp, like, and he went nearly crazy trying to be macho, to look and sound well hard. He was keen as mustard (not keen as buggery, don't even go there!), and pretty fit and pretty strong and always up for anything, no problem there at all. But everywhere he went they all made kissing noises, and the sound of plungers sucking out of blocked up sewage pipes, and spat at him and called him fag and poof and queer and fudge packer and the rest of it. On the range one day Sarnt Williams was thrashing another bloke and told him to do fifty push-ups. Then, before he'd started, he told this gay lad to lie face downwards under him to "keep him hard at work!" We all laughed like drains, but not long after he went unit, then got out. Depression.

That's how Jamal went, come to think of it. When Shahid was with him he got on fine, 'cause no one dared with Sha, but on his own he got the Paki this and Paki that treatment, and it seemed to get him down. The NCOs were just as bad as usual, and one day he went for one of them, a skinny dim lancejack from Huddersfield, and they had a little scuffle before some lads pulled Jamal off and booted him about a bit, but it was Jam that got the book thrown at him. According to Shahid, the OC said he had to try harder to fit in, and if he thought the lance corporal had made a racist remark he was wrong, it was a "misinterpretation." Then he gave him a little lecture on equality, and said it was Jamal who'd been picking on the lance in fact, because he had a "vulnerable position" and could lose his stripe! I.e., Jam had done it on purpose to get the poor lad busted! Jamal held on three weeks after that. Then it was unit. Depression. Out.

And everyone was happy. A result.

The most boring part of helping new recruits, for my money, was teaching them how to wash and clean their teeth, and iron shirts and do up buttons and so on. When I hit Catterick, I thought the piss was being taken, big style, when my sergeant asked how many of us had a toothbrush. But it was Big Knob, who I'd already worked out on Day Two was not so bad, and you could tell he meant it. Everyone said they had, but you could also tell that lots of them were lying, they looked at everybody else to see what the question meant and what the answer ought to be. I went in with about sixty other kids – I was the oldest, on account of university – and a good six of them had never cleaned their teeth. They got issued with a toothbrush (and charged later, I expect), and we had a lickle dem-onstration. Today, with Sarnt Williams, that was my job. Wet the fucking brush, put on the toothpaste from the tube, wiggle up and down, and spit. Yeah, Dumbo! Spit! Don't swallow it. Then rinse and spit again. Then wash the brush and screw the cap back on the tube. Do that every day and your Ma might want to kiss you, for the first time in your life.

You think I'm joking, don't you – go on, admit it, my mum did. No joke. Some of these poor bastards, judging by the smell, didn't even know you had to wipe your arse. So maybe that's the good bit, then. Look at some of these poor fuckers twelve months later, and they're fit, and proud, and civilised enough to get blown to pieces by an IED. Look out you terrorists, here we come. England's finest.

Ironing a shirt, shaving properly, blowing your nose, washing, having a shower. All this I went through, all this I played the sergeant's guinea pig to show. I was from Blackburn, he told everyone, where we didn't have running water yet, or flushing toilets, and you used your sleeve to wipe your nose on, and your girlfriend's knickers after intercourse, if she was posh enough to wear 'em (and know the meaning of that word). Even the lads from Blackburn fell about, especially when he asked if there were any Muslims in, despite the fact that everyone in the room was white.

"We're completely racially tolerant in the army," he said, "so I've got to ask. Just 'cause you ain't Paki-coloured don't mean you ain't a Moslem, and Moslems gob on the ground a lot, which squaddies, believe you me, do not." Pause. "Not unless you want your bollocks nailing to the floor, d'you get me?"

After dinner, towards the end of the afternoon, I was feeling really knackered. It was probably the last night's booze, but my mum had always told me "brainwork," as she called what she did, was just as hard or harder than "honest labour." I might have given her the benefit of the doubt, except it would've meant that officers did real work too, and that was bollocks, obviously. All the officers in the training unit were so *nice*, so absolutely bleeding useless, so desperate to be fair, and "normal" and be liked. But they weren't, of course, it was the sergeants who ran the show, and their opinion of the flathats was diabolical. They were toffs, they were rich stuck-up bastards who earned a fortune and knew fuck all, and lots of 'em had stupid toffy accents, to put the lid on it. Figures of fun, that was the most respect they got. Figures of fun and hatred. No respect at all.

Case in point – on the last session of the afternoon an officer was in, all beaming smiles and encouragement. This bloke was a lieutenant, bit old, bit podgy, bit useless or he'd've got promotion, wouldn't he? He give a little talk about the history of the army, how we were there to help these people (he didn't say exactly who, but let's guess the Afghans shall we, except the Taliban, ho ho) and "the goal for every soldier is to bring the gift of peace." I felt Ken's brandy rising in my throat, and my eyes were flashing in the sunshine and the heat, and I'm like – Jesus, did I get this bullshit shot at me last year? Did I hear it all and not throw up? It must be brainwashing. It must be something in the tea. We must be idiots.

Then after he'd spoke, and the CSM had had a go, Sarnt Williams hit me with his masterstroke. I was sitting in a total daze, head banging, and he must have said my name a dozen times before it sunk into my skull.

"Hassan!" he was going. "Hassan! Are you receiving me? Earth to Tiny Hassan! I'm sorry, sir, I warned everyone he was from Black-burn, but this is... We call him Tiny because he ain't too bright. Soft-lad!! Hassan!!!"

The whole room was falling about, and the officer, thank God, was joining in the fun. But then I felt a bit pissed off, I got resentful. Everyone was laughing, the day outside was fine and sweet, and my mates were in the country in the south, not long till knockoff time, beer, curry, river, girls. And here was I, Williams's whipping post, his bitch. So bollocks to the lot of them.

"Well, I'm not sure if you've chosen the right man, Sergeant," the lieutenant was wittering, "but at least the new boys'll get the true authentic voice of squaddie-dom! Lads, I give you Private 'Tiny' Hassan. He'll tell you how we live here day-to-day. Thank you, Hassan. Continue."

Continue? What, continue blinking? I looked at Williams and his face was a picture of contented spite.

"Go on, la'," he said, after a short wait. "Cat get your tongue, did 'e? Give the lads a lecture. Tell it like it is!"

But without the swear words, naturally. Without the nasty bits, the truth. I looked at all the pasty bastards sitting there, the sweepings off the classroom floor, the kids who wouldn't ever get a proper job, and I felt really sorry for them. Then I nearly laughed.

"Sir?" I said, to the officer. "Is that right, sir? Tell it like it is?"

I saw the sergeant's gob open but the lieutenant got there first.

"Why not?" he said. "Just a normal day, for once. Just a flavour of our life here in the garrison. Catterick, men, is a really special place."

I spose I bottled it in a way. I felt this great big surge inside me, and the first word that rose up was fuck. Well it would be in the

121

army, wouldn't it? It fucking would be. But something stopped me. I glanced at the lieutenant's face again, smiling happily, and I felt sorry for *him*, an' all. Now what's *that* about? I felt sorry for a dickhead officer.

"Six thirty, half past six," I said. I sounded like a speak-your-weight machine. "Get up, the crack of dawn, and do the block jobs. Well, have a shower first and get dressed. Yeah, some people shower every day, your skin don't fall off, honest. Then after block jobs—"

A hand went up in the front row. Jesus, keen bastard, eh?

"Please, er... Mister... Mate..."

"Dickhead," said Williams, absent-mindedly.

"Sergeant!" went the officer, eyebrows raised but still smiling. "Good question, though. Private? Block jobs?"

"You know," I said. "Jobs on the block. It might be, like... washing the showers out. Er, sweeping up. Mopping floors."

"General tidying," said the lieutenant. "Is that it, Private? General clearing up."

"Yeah, well," I said. "I mean, yes, sir. Well, like everybody's meant to clear their own crap up and take it to the skips but that don't last for long. Most people just chuck it in the corridors, in bin bags if you're lucky, because they know someone's got to do it. Sergeants are worst, and lancejacks next. Whatever Sarnt Williams here wants you to believe."

That was a try-on, just to see what happened, and everybody laughed their socks off. Williams put on a laugh as well, but his eyes were after mine like heat-seeking missiles, which I avoided by grinning at the officer, who grinned back. Normally these talks are boring, pointless. Normally by now the recruits would be asleep. I suppose it made some sort of sense to him.

"Oh, I forgot," I said. "Before the corridors you've got to do the bogs. You know, clean up the porno mags stuffed down behind the toilets and rub off the crystallised piss all round the bowls." I nearly mentioned needles but I thought he'd only stand so much. I bet he'd never seen a squaddies' bog, I bet he'd not believe it, stupid prat. Let alone the shit smeared on the walls.

"Hassan," said Williams, struggling to keep his cool. "Don't get too daft, will you, la'? Don't tear the...bottom out of it."

This got another laugh out of the crap-hats, because the word was "arse" and everybody knew it. Another laugh, another nail banged in my coffin. But the lieutenant still didn't seem to be pissed off. Smiling like a fool, in fact. I blundered on.

"Anyway," I said, "that's the best part of the day over. Downhill all the way now – it's breakfast time. The only good thing is that not many people bother going, because we have PT next, so what's the point? The more you eat, the more there is to run off, ain't there? And the fuller up your guts are, the worse it feels." I grinned out at them. They were sitting there dead interested, probably wondering how much of it was true, and why I was allowed to say it, anyway. "Best reason not to go I've left till last," I said. "It's like eating shite. It's diabolical."

"That's pretty cynical!" said the lieutenant, almost fucking giggling. "He's 'playing the old soldier,' is what my colonel used to call it, but it's a point of view so I won't censor him!"

Sarnt Williams would've, if he'd been able to. Sarnt Williams would have killed me. I'd got the taste though. What could they do to me? More punishment? Bollocks to 'em.

"PT, then," I said. "One hour, two, depending on how the sergeants feel that morning. It's usually a TAB or a boot run or maybe circuits. If you're in Sarnt Williams's company you're fucked, because—"

I had to stop then, because there was a gale of laughs and shouting. Shocked, they were, pretending to be scandalised. It's funny, innit – swearing in front of an officer was the big taboo, it was like farting in front of the Queen or some bloody bishop. But officers swear, I've heard them, and anyway they must do, it stands to reason – like the Queen must lay a good stiff shit from time to time. But I must admit I'd shocked myself, thrown myself out of synch. Not least because the sergeant's look was black and stormy, like a bloody hurricane. I'm not stupid. I went for the recovery.

"I'm sorry, sir," I said, "that just slipped out. The reason you don't want to be in the sergeant's company is not because you're...you know...but because it's the best, the boss company, so if you're lazy, like I am, you get thrashed worse than in the others. The fat blokes

124

all end up at the back, and the rest of us get beasted because we should make sure that everybody's fit. D'you get it? If some bugger can't run, or won't run, it's your fault, all of you. And everybody hates the Jock bastards, because they don't even try."

Maybe I shouldn't have said that, because it sounded a bit like racism, and officers are very hot on that in theory, in case there's anybody listening. But Williams approved, and the lieutenant didn't notice, far too thick. So thick in fact I got another little dig in.

"It's worst in winter obviously," I said. "Okay now, but in January they make you parade outside your CHQ and stand still in your shorts for hours. You can see the officers and senior NCOs inside, having a laugh at you and drinking tea. It's worse though if you're fat and podgy like I said, because then they take the piss as well. If you're unhealthy, see, it's bad. People look down on you."

I looked at all the pasty faces and got a big smile on my mush.

"The best thing if you really do it hard, is that you feel good," I said. "After the graft the pay-off. Back in the shower for a good long time, hot water, steam and a bucketful of gel. I got switched on dead early when I joined – I always had ironed DPMs and polished boots to get into. Do 'em the night before, it makes you feel great, no shit. Oops, sorry sir. There I go again!"

He looked at me like a friendly teacher (if these kids had ever seen one, which wasn't likely when you think about it), and waved his hand like I should carry on. I was on a roll. I was enjoying it.

"After that you've got an hour to yourself, more if you're crafty, like. Nine thirty shower, change, and then sit in your room and play computer games, or watch Ballamory if you're a real sad bastard, there's no one in England knows more about kids' and daytime telly crap than squaddies, you can win pub quizzes on it. Then at eleven someone comes and says 'what you on?' And you say 'Oh, I've got to go and see Lieutenant Blah, or the dentist, or the clerks about me pay,' and at half past, maybe, someone else says 'Warrior crews to report to garage after scoff,' so then you've got to work out another reason, like a brain tumour or a heart attack, to keep you sitting on your arse. I'm telling you, it's a hard life. Thank God we get well-paid!"

Wasn't there *nothing* I could say to rile this twat lieutenant? The kids were rolling in the aisles and he was smiling like Father fucking Christmas. I didn't dare to look at Sarnt Williams, there was no percentage there, no way. I just enjoyed the laughing and the whoops and cheers. I'd never spoke like this before about the army. I'd never told it like it was. Not to me mother, anyway. Not to her in any way at all.

"Lunch," I said. "Let's say burgers pie and chips. Baguette on the side, with rice and extra bread and butter. And more chips. There's salad – there's even pictures of it on the walls, to show it's good for you – but I've never seen no-one actually eat any, it's fucking rabbit food. Then from thirteen hundred on you sit around a bit, play football if you're any good and get pissed on from a great height if you aren't, then from fourteen thirty, that's half past two in English, an NCO might try and nab you for a job, unless you can dodge again. Everybody loves that, don't they Sarge?"

I risked a look at him and his eyes were fucking gimlets, willing me to die. The NCOs are there to keep you keen, see – if you ain't, it's them that's failures. I was digging him deeper and deeper in the shite, and the trogs were loving it. They were delirious. And he couldn't make me stop. He was completely bolloxed.

"Anyway," I said, "sometimes they've got you skewered, haven't they? Say I'm on CFT Warrior – sent down to the garage, full checks, right? But even that's not too bad when you get used to it, is it? There's ways and means."

The lieutenant was looking interested, so I pulled back a bit. Didn't want to drop *me* in it as well, did I? I winked at them, my "audience," out of his line of sight.

"Course, this isn't me that's talking now 'cause I'm a good boy, but there's some awful skivers, Sergeant Williams'll back me up, it makes his life a ruddy misery sometimes. Let's say it works like this. This squaddie – anyone but me – gets sent down to do full checks, but he doesn't have a clue. The other driver might know what he's doing, it's just possible, but he's fast asleep in the back, hung over. So the squad-die looks around to find out if the Colour's lurking, and if he ain't, he does a crafty bunk. Hide in me room until parade and fall-out – then fill up on scoff again. After that the meatheads go back to the gym, the pissheads hit the pubs – not an option for you lot, yet – and the bad boys do some smoking in their room, know what I mean, nudge nudge? Keen lads like you'll box up your kit, polish your boots for morning, and that's you squared away. The night is young and Cat-terick's stretched out like a... like a..."

I fell about all of a sudden. I lost it. Like a pile of diamonds, or a pile of horse manure? Oh Catterick, world capital of the Shit Night Out! The boggin' slags, you wouldn't touch 'em with a bargepole. The Kingo hardmen in the pubs, the Jocks sky high on crack, the Yorkies saving money, the Scousers nicking it, and everywhere the crowds of scruffy civvy wankers, as miserable as prisoners of war. Then all get drunk and back to bed as pissed as arseholes, night after night after fucking night. I'd stopped laughing. It wasn't really funny any more.

"You can go to the gym, of course," I said. "You don't have to go out drinking, there's lots to do around the camp, there's got to be, ain't there? Then in the morning...SSDD."

"I know that one," said the lieutenant, proud as Punch, the daft soft sod. "It means Same Shit, Different Day. And I say Private Hassan deserves a clap for that talk, chaps, don't you? Cynical but stimulating! Well done, Private Hassan!"

He started, and poor old Williams joined in as well, he had no choice, did he? Christ, that must have hurt. I managed to avoid him in the crush to reach the canteen, because Lieutenant Bonehead wanted to have a word with him. I actually heard him congratulate him, on *my* "performance." It was rough, he said, raw, a wee bit cheeky – but "pretty darn authentic."

Yeah, thanks a bunch, I thought. Plenty there for Sarnt Williams to pay me back for. Oh Jesus – was I going to suffer.

Four

I got a call from Sha that night, from Sha and Ashton down in the soft south. I was feeling pretty pissed off anyway – and hung over from mad old Ken next door – and it didn't bloody help, no way. They sounded high as kites, and Ash was up to his old giggling. Sha said the crack was excellent, the weather was fantastic and they were "really, *really* missing you, know wha' ah mean, ya wankah!"

Fuck off, I thought, that's all I need, me best mates turning gay. Oh yeah, I said, pull the other one, why don't you, it's got bells on.

"No seriously," he said, "you're doing a great job up there, ain't you? Keep an eye on him, keep the bugger in your sights. We've only got a few weeks more down here, then we'll have the bastard proper."

"What bugger? What bastard? What the fuck you on about, Shahid? The only job I'm doing is getting in the shit. What you on about?"

"Goughie," he said. "The great big streak of yellow piss. He's been telling people you beat up a cop girl. That's why you got busted back. He's been on the phone to Bollocks Bowyer. He's been telling people I'm a fucking terrorist!"

"You fucking are!" goes Ashton in the background. "Osama Bin Liner, you fucking Paki twat!"

"I'll stick a rocket up your arse if you ain't careful," Shahid told him. "Listen, Tiny, what do you think? That ginger SAS bloke that went on the train with you is definitely an undercover man, Goughie told Bollocks. And Goughie's told him everything. Straight up."

"But I didn't hit the cop girl! It was the Colour! Fucking Goughie saw it! I was with him! Why would he say that?"

"Because it's true!" went Ashton. "Confess! Repent! Sing halleebleedinglujah!"

"Ash," said Sha, "fuck off. This is serious. Look, I've got a strawberry condom in me pocket. Go and get some tart to suck it for you."

"But I didn't hit her, Sha," I said. "I fucking didn't, he *knows* it. What did Bollocks say to him?"

Bollocks, apparently, had told Goughie he was barking, and liable to lose his face. But Bollocks was a friend of Martie, wasn't he, so Martie would get fed the stupid tale in any case. That was Sha's theory.

"Yeah," I said. "Sounds dead on to me. But no one's going to believe it off of Goughie, are they? I mean – you a terrorist! You joined the fucking *army*!"

"Yeah, and I did it for the cover, didn't I? Even I can see how that would sound. I'm a Muslim, therefore I'm a terrorist, so I join the army and no one'll know. To the Intelligence Branch that probably sounds intelligent, and to put the tin lid on it, I'm always eating bacon and hanging round outside Mecca drinking lemonade and praying."

"You don't drink lemonade," went Ashton. "You drink like a fucking fish."

"I don't play bingo either, you prat! Or pray to Allah, come to that! Ashton – *go away!*"

Sha wasn't really worried, in the end, he'd just rung up to have a laugh. But it explained why Gough was avoiding me, I spose, and I wondered if there'd be any comeback. I tell you what though – next time I saw him he'd get my toecap up his arse.

Next time I did see him, in fact, was quite a long time after, when the trogs had been trained up enough to fire a live round on the ranges. I was Williams's sidekick as per usual, and all us spare squaddies were there for safety, like, to "keep an eye on things." It wasn't dangerous, though, they were always telling us there'd never been an accident, and quite honestly, most new kids thought it was the funfair, with real guns and bullets to make it pretty cool. Plus the added bonus there was lots of live rounds lying in the dirt to take home to impress your mates and family afterwards.

Sarnt Williams was showing off as usual, and beasting me to show he was the boss. He'd got them all sat down in rows, and lectured them on how guns could kill you and crap like that, and when it

131

wan't their turn they had to be like cunts in a kindergarten, not move a fucking muscle.

"Most of all, no talking, yeah? I want dead silence or some one of you'll end up really dead, geddit? See that range-flag over there? Well if you talk, you crawl to it on your belly, then fucking back again. You don't believe me? Hassan! Come 'ead and tell 'em 'ow it's fucking true!"

I was sitting on me arse but I got up to answer, I knew his funny little ways. Oh no I didn't though. I wasn't even fully on me feet before he screamed at me in a mock rage dragged up from nowhere. Hopping up and down, he was. What a bastard.

"Are you takin' the piss, Hassan?" he yelled. "Do I look like I've got all day! Well you can give us a demo can't you, you fucking asked for it! Range flag – go!"

They were all goggling at me, half-smiling at the sergeant's fun because they had to, and I noticed the one called Jeff, his "Al Bino," was the only squaddie there who showed no interest. I'd noticed already that he was pretty miserable these days, and the night before, old Ken had told me why. It turned out that his "mother," the one that he'd been fool enough to say had bought his coat for him, wasn't his real mum after all, she was a sort of carer. He'd been in a kid's home till eleven, then farmed out into foster, and it was round the camp like wildfire. He was "Billy No-Mum," now, or "Little Orphan Annie." He was "such a fucking loser, his folks gave him away."

"Well," said the sergeant. "What you waiting for? Go! Not on your legs, you twat! *Crawl*, you knob-end! *Crawl!*"

In my best combats too. Creases like knives. Boots bulled up to buggery. I crawled. It was when I reached the range flag I saw Goughie, over with another lot of trogs on another section, and I had my choice. He'd been avoiding me like mad, and there he was – so I could either shout out the big hello from Sha and Ashton to show I knew what he'd been up to, or I could let him get away with it. If I shouted and Williams heard, I was in the shit. If I said nowt, how would he know I knew?

Logistics. Tactics. Easy. I went on one elbow as I crawled, and made like I were flipping open a mobile, and clamped it to my ear and sneered at him. Then I snapped it shut (my fist), and pulled a finger across my throat, like a butcher's knife. All done in deadly silence, and even Goughie, thick as pigshit, would get the message. But he'd seen me crawling, he'd seen me being beasted by the sergeant, and he couldn't keep the smile off of his face. Right, you twat, just keep on fucking smiling. A knife across the neck won't be the fucking half of it.

The rest of the range-time was just boring. It was the crap-hats' first go at it, so they were interested for a while, like you always are, but it soon wears off. Ashton reckons that if all the English "Yardie twats," the would-be Jamaica gunmen, the black doods and rapper-men who make it impossible for a "good class niggah" to walk down the street without a stop'n search – if all of them was given guns at school, by the time they was eleven they'd be bored titless of the fucking boring things. I can strip down an SA80 in three seconds in the pitch black dark with six fingers up my arse. And if I never saw another one again it would be much too bleeding soon.

One little laugh at dinner-break, though, if you like that sort of thing. There were two veggies in this new mob – two who admitted it anyway, slow learners – and when the "range poo" containers were opened up, the only stuff the cooks had sent out for them to eat was leftover veg from yesterday. One of the daft bastards, a Wigan lad, dared to half-complain, so the sergeant tipped it out onto the grass, for both of them. Then his lancejack got out some spare cheese sandwiches, and made the veggies reach for them. They never got close enough though, did they? Sandwiches on ground, boots on sandwiches, "apologies" all round. Ooh, how we all giggled at his brilliant sense of humour. I tell you, it's like watching savages. It's like watching people with no brains.

I did another piss-up with old Ken that night, and asked him what he thought of the army, honestly. I went into his room to do it, and I took a bottle of brandy that I'd gone down and got at Tesco's. He was sitting on his bed in a pair of tatty boxers, fat as a Buddha wreathed in smoke, and about half pissed already. I went in cautious, in case I wasn't welcome, but he didn't give a bugger, you could tell.

He raised a buttock first, to ease one out, and just said "You married are you, Hassan?" as if we'd been in the middle of a conversation.

I shook my head, but didn't answer. I'd had a text off Bridgie earlier as it happened, asking for the money that I owed her, lying cow. I waved me bottle at him, opened it, and found a cup for me. His

guitar was on the floor beside his bed, but he was doing nowt when I
went in. Twiddling his thumbs.

"Bleeding right too, son," he said, "you keep it that way. It don't
go together in my experience, marriage and the army." He took a
drink, and coughed. He sucked on his cigarette till the filter went
red hot and nearly melted. He coughed some more, and dropped
the dog-end in an ashtray, where it smoked and stank. He laughed.

"Marriage and anything, in actual fact," he said. "Men and women,
that's the problem. Without them two ingredients it would be a
damn good thing all round. We're incompatible."

"I won't get married, Ken," I said. "I can guarantee it. No normal
girl would even look at me."

His belly jigged about a bit at that, and he lit another fag.

"No guarantee at all, that ain't," he said. "There ain't no normal
girls in Catterick to start with, they're so desperate they'll fuck
anything that moves. It's the wives you want to go for, though, the
wives are easy, ask your Uncle Ken. The secret is to screw 'em when
the old man's posted, and drop 'em fast when Johnnie comes marching home again. Deny everything, and if anyone gets hurt it isn't
you. Are you with me?"

Not really, but what do I know, eh? Sure as shit unfaithful didn't
mean a thing to Bridgie, and if I got hurt, well fuck my luck. But
Ken had lost his interest now. He'd picked up his guitar and was
strumming through the last verse of a song I'd heard before. A
soldier's song about a lad that's buggered off and left his wife and

kid to starve while he goes finding glory. And then comes marching home again. Well, not exactly marching…

> *You haven't an arm and you haven't a leg,*
> *Haroo, haroo.*
> *You haven't an arm and you haven't a leg,*
> *Haroo.*
> *You haven't an arm and you haven't a leg,*
> *You're an eyeless, noseless, chickenless egg.*
> *You'll have to sit out with a bowl and beg –*
> *Johnnie I hardly knew ya.*

It was a brilliant tune, and the words were fucking awful, when you thought about it. An eyeless, noseless, chickenless egg. Christ. Cooked up inside a Warrior that's caught an RPG. You could see it in his face, what Ken Rogers thought. It seemed to say it all for him.

"I did four years in Northern Ireland when I were your age," he said, when he'd finished. He put the guitar down and picked up his fag, and smoked it quietly for a good long while. "I drove Land Rovers, it was easy in them days, they were a good tool for the job – in and out quick as a flash, and the IRA bullets rattled off the armour, even MG rounds. We still use 'em now against the Taliban, and they can blow 'em inside out for fun. They're bastards, Tiny, and I don't mean the enemy. They've thrown us to the wolves, mate. They do not give a flying farting fuck."

His mood was moving to the black again, any fool could see that. And I didn't have a thing to say. We knew all about our weapons and equipment, we talked about them all the time. We knew that we were being lied to.

"I drive a Warrior," I said. "Good tool."

"Yeah. Good tool. Good tomb. Good luck, Sunny Jim. You'll fucking need it."

What could I do? I couldn't get up and just walk out, could I? But he was sinking pretty fast. He lifted up his mug and drank like it was water. Then he filled it up again.

"D'you know what they used to call us when I went to Iraq?" he said. He raised his face and focused on my eyes. "They called us the Borrowers. The Yankee soldiers did. They thought we were pathetic, and they give us everything, they're generous, the Yanks, incredible."

He stopped. He coughed. He carried on.

"Our issue boots were crap, they melted in the heat," he said, "so the Yanks bought Spanish, then passed them on to us, proper bastard boots that didn't let the sand in. We didn't have no night goggles, no body armour, no radios that worked, no creams and lotions for sore eyes and bollocks, no proper fucking tents, so the Yankees give us everything, or sold it if they didn't want to show us up. The country fucking cousins, eh? Jesus, I spent most of my pay on non-issue gear, and some storemen even stock it in our stores now, so they can take an extra fucking cut! And all the time in Parliament the lying bastards say that our kit's wonderful, the very very best. We used to sit and pray, sometimes. That they'd send some politician out to war, John Reid or Hoon, or that funny little fucker with the Hitler moustache. Just for a week. In British gear. In a snatch Land Rover. With an SA fucking 80."

Down goes another cup of brandy. Maybe he'd drink himself to death. Maybe I would, ditto. He blinked at me. I smiled.

"SA80. What d'you think of it? Okay rifle is it?" he said. "Not that you've ever fired one up to your balls in red hot sand, I spose."

I hadn't. Please God I'd never have to, neither.

"First ten years in service it was scrap," he said. "British designed, British developed, British built, unusable. When I first started, our lives were on the line day after fucking day because it wouldn't work. Would they admit it? You tell me. It had to be dragged out of them, disaster after disaster, cock-ups galore, until you could hear the bastards lying right across the world – it was the future, it was wonderful, it was the very best. Fire it twice, it jammed. Dust, sand, damp, garlic on the fucking breath, it wouldn't fire. They lied, and lied, and lied and fucking lied. And when the game was up, they got it redesigned and built by Germans, all hush-hush. Good tool now." He took another swallow of his brandy. Had another cough. He looked at me.

"How much did you have to spend on proper gear then, when you joined?" he asked. "Can you put a figure on it?"

I said nothing, but I knew it was all true. I remembered how it was last year, and I knew damn well it hadn't changed. The storemen kept the good stuff alongside the issue, and the choice was yours. Spend money, or freeze to death, or boil, or get pneumonia and trenchfoot from the damp. Gordon Broon's Fashion Accessories the storemen used to call the proper gear, although I'm fucked if I know

what they call it now that cunt's been forgotten. It's a scandal really.
A complete dis-fucking-grace.

But it was time to go, at last. No answer needed after all, because
Ken was now unconscious, or asleep. His mouth was open, his dog-
end drowned in dribble, his plastic mug all nestled in his hairy tits.
I didn't tuck him up or give him a kiss goodnight, surprise surprise.
It was bayonets in the morning. Five bloody thirty up. That was
enough shit to be going on with. More than enough.

Five

Only a complete pillock would have gone on the piss the night before a bayonet day, so you can work that out yourself. I wasn't being trained, of course, and nor were Williams's lot in theory – new trogs don't get bayonet till Week Thirteen or so. But the fact he'd swapped duties with another sergeant so he could be part of it should have been warning enough for me to lay off drinking. Williams wanted fun. And he wanted fun at my expense, an' all.

He kicked into my room at five o'clock and this time didn't bother just dragging me covers off. Before I was even half awake he gripped the bed frame under me and heaved it so I smashed onto the floor, then let it go so that it crashed down again and bounced. My side locker went over, a glass of water and my alarm went flying, and Williams shouted: "Get up, get up, get up, you cunt! I told you five o'clock!"

He'd told me half-past five, but what the fuck, no arguing. I forced myself to jump up to my feet and this time I had underpants on at least, because I'd guessed he'd pull some sort of stunt.

"Floor Three!" he yelled. "We've got Tankie's lot! I want them all out and in their gear ready for inspection at five thirty five!"

Oh yeah, likely. They'd not been warned or anything the night before – part of the technique was to keep them guessing till they actually saw the dummies hanging there – but if I didn't get them moving the shit would hit the fan, for *me*. I was halfway dressed before he even left my room, and I heard him banging on Ken's door to wake him up too, the spiteful bastard. Ken was on the sick, remember – offically bonkers, declared unfit to even look at a loaded rifle let alone have hold of one – so drag him down the ranges with us, that's army humour. When I got down to Sergeant Tankerton's lines his corporals were already on the rampage, it was a bear garden. Squaddies were racing through their block jobs, kicking over mop buckets, swinging brooms, and in every room you could hear shouting and swearing and beasting, big time.

The general idea some sergeants had of bayonet training was a sort of throwback to them films you see about the war. Big Knob reckoned it was psychology – to drive lads into a frenzy of fear and hate to make them realise what it would be like to fight somebody hand-to-hand – and he refused to do it. He said it was stupid, because people who could go mental would go mental anyway, they didn't need play-acting, and the rest of us would "learn it on the night – or die." Sarnt Williams, though, surprise surprise, was a wind-'em-up-till-their-eyeballs-popped merchant. He loved bayonet training. He got his rocks off on it.

My job was to back up Williams, and his job, as he saw it, was to beef up some of the corporals, who might be soft. The best way, in his view, was to reduce the recruits (not crap-hats any more, they'd passed off the square) to jelly, and to make them exhausted before they even got out to the fields. At first we barged into their rooms, shouting if they weren't in their combats, shouting if they were, messing up their beds if they'd got them made already, the whole general thrashing routine. Then they got three minutes to muster outside in the corridors in full gear, "parade ground smart," and anything, real or not real, would do to send them back, to come out again in PT kit. Once out in shorts they'd get blasted back again to "dress proper," and if they took too long – three minutes, say – they'd start it all again, with press-ups thrown in for a bonus. Some of them were as hungover as I was, on account they weren't trogs no more so could drink in the Naafi or go out into town, and he targeted them the worst.

The canteen opened at six o'clock on bayonet days, but the idea was to give them fifteen minutes for their breakfast, then make them too late to eat it, like. That was easy – when their uniform was right, you told them it was wrong, and go the fuck and change it. Other groups got off earlier than ours, so by the time we got to the canteen there were ten minutes left and queues from here to Kingdom Come. The food was shite in any case, so people didn't mind not eating it, except that they'd get damn all else until some evil bastard (Sarnt Williams) said they could have their dinner on the ranges, and you know what Bob Marley said about an 'ungry man. His dad was in the British Army too. And a fucking Scouser! So my lot copped for breakfast right at the complete last minute, and before they'd got a mouthful down Williams screamed at me to scream at them to get it in the swill and get their arses back outside.

"Too slow!" he shouted, as the last few stumbled out. "Frog hops, the lot of you! That building over there! Yeah, thass right, the fuck-ing lot of you! If you've been waiting don't blame me! Blame your so-called mates for keeping you! They've done it on purpose, can't you work that out? They fucking hate you, that's why! Your fucking

mates'd fucking kill you if they had the chance! You've missed your
breakfast. Frog hops!"

Squaddies are like politicians. When in doubt plead ignorance and
hope you'll be all right, you could see it in their faces. They didn't
know what frog hops were, they'd never heard of them they said,
which was bollocks but it must be worth a try. So guess what happens now?

"Hassan! They've never heard of frogs! They don't know how the
little fuckers jump! Show 'em, Hassan! That firehose and back!
Yeah, that one, la'. *Now!*"

It's hard work, frog-hopping, it's a killer. No way of faking, neither.
Toes out, heels together, hands clasped behind your back. And
every hop, your body's got to go right down between your open
knees, then you bounce up again, like a puppet on a spring. About
two hundred metres I had to go, and Williams made me do it on
my own, so that "they" could see me. So that he could, more like,
so that I couldn't use the other bastards to shield me if I eased the
bounces off or moved my hands in front. When it started raining
I took it as a sign that God existed after all, although the others
thought he was a bastard. But it was cool, and the alcohol in my
blood was on the boil. I reckon you could of bottled my sweat and
sold it to the Jocks.

When I got back to them I was glowing like a red hot stove, half
blind with rain and sweat. I'd got the hang of the sergeant now, so I
didn't get to my feet until he told me to, because I didn't fancy frog-
ging there and back again. I got reprieved, and the other bastards
gave me dirty looks when he told them to go without me, as if I was

getting off of something! They did it in batches, split into threes, and while the first lot hopped off, the other two thirds marched on the spot or took up the usual range of stress positions, with me to check if they unbent their legs and arms or tried to put one foot down or any con like that. I must say their faces were filling up with hatred pretty fast, which was the whole point in the sergeant's warped mind. There were always fights in Catterick after bayonet days, in the camp and in the town. I made a note of the best ones to avoid if I was going drinking later on. Not that I thought I would be. I thought that I might rather die.

An hour and a half all this went on, and by that time some blokes were almost fizzing, you could see it. Then it was "collect rifles," with constant harrying and yelling, and once you'd got yours it was line up again then break off in groups and run round and round the parade ground with your SA80 held above your head, both arms, intermixed with press-ups, stress positions, and marching on the spot. After that they were all formed up and marched off the actual barracks through a gate that led out to the fields, where – surprise surprise – there was a hill they could be beasted on, marching up it, running up it, hopping up it, crawling up it, sheer blue bloody fucking murder.

The dummies were in lines on sort of gantries – a gallows was the real idea – with some in one row, some in the row behind, and so on. The method was to rush down screaming, skewer a dummy from arsehole to breakfast-time, then charge on to the next one, still screaming like a schizo on a big day out.

Before the charge you had to fix your bayonet – out of webbing, on to flash eliminator, twist, check – which struck me as the danger part. The rifles weren't loaded, but some of the lads were, they'd have stabbed their Auntie Mabel given half a chance. Some of them were damn near foaming at the mouth.

"You're going to kill 'em!" Sergeant Williams screamed. "It's life and death, you poke cold steel or die yourself! It's not an easy death, it's not a bullet or a nice big bloody bang, it's a piece of rusty, twisty metal stained with your best mate's blood. They're going to kill you! They're going to turn your mother inside out, and rape your sister, they're going to force-feed you camel shit and curry! And they don't drink alcohol, they're not human! So kill the bastards! Kill! Kill! Kill!"

I swear to God that most of them had swallowed it. They raced off down the slope screaming and bellowing, and stabbed and tore and dragged out in a frenzy. Not everyone. I saw two or three lads who looked sick, embarrassed, who felt they were being proper fools, pretending. That's how I always was, when I was trained to do it. Every three weeks, or a month or so, I went through the motions, the big lie, and I wondered how I'd be if I ever had to do it for real. Dead, I guess. Or maybe cool and calm and dead effective. Who knows?

I remembered one thing, though. The gay lad, who'd been mocked and hit and bullied till he went unit and went crawling back to mum – he'd been a dervish at the bayonet field. He'd been like a whirlwind of hatred, frothing at the mouth. Maybe that's the answer. Get the enemy to call you bumboy, or treat you like a fairy, and you'll stab their tripes out and drink their pissing blood. Oh yeah. Psychology.

"You're rubbish!" shouted Sarnt Williams as they staggered out the other end. "You're dead! You're like a gang of fucking poofs. D'you want a bayonet with a girlie-button, is that it? D'you want one with a bunch of roses at the end? On the spot! March! And you six – press-ups! Go on, faster! Faster! Put some fucking balls in it, you wankers!"

As the next lot came off he abused them too, and then the next lot, until there was room at the start again. The marchers on the spot were then shot round to go again, then the push-up gang, while the latest team to stagger off were thrashed and beasted in their turn. The screaming at the dummies was constant, it never stopped, and the teams went round and round and round and got madder and madder and madder, far as I could see. The yells were hate-ist, sexist, racist, gayist, you name it-ist. Even I was shaky, and I hadn't done a thing. And after three hours Williams called a halt to have some scran. For fifteen bleeding minutes. Just fifteen.

There were fights and scuffles from now on, nothing serious, but the sergeants and corporals didn't try to break them up unless they looked like going OTT. On the march back to barracks at the end there was more trouble, and most people missed their food and went straight off for a shower then to the Naafi or the outside pubs. There were punch-ups in the showers, then in the laundry and the drying rooms, because lots of blokes' clean gear that they'd done earlier had been nicked from off the hangers as usual. You could smell it in the air, like tigers in the zoo. There'd be trouble in Catterick later on, for certain. No wonder the locals were like Shaun and the fucking dead.

When I got back to the lines with Sergeant Williams, though, things got much worse, faster than the speed of light. The place was buzzing, with older squaddies, NCOs, RMPs, even officers inside the block. Something must have happened, and the Sarnt raced off to get the lowdown off his mates, and left me to it. No one was saying much that made a lot of sense, but I worked out soon enough that someone had shot himself – and not one of our official lunatics, because I saw two of them ghosting round the corridors, and the other one had been carted off by the men in white just the day before.

And then I got it, and it made me go completely sick. Ken had been on the ranges, barking mad or not – and Ken had not come back. He'd been in a total state last night, pissed up, passed out, and he'd been going on about women, wives, the government, the bleeding lot. He'd not seemed suicidal, but what the fuck did I know? It was Ken.

I don't know what was going off with me. I tell you straight I ran back to my room and fucking cried. I sat down on that fucking awful bed and fucking howled, like a little baby. I'd done it once before, when my grandad died, and that had shocked me, too, because he was just a nice old git, but not my best mate in the world or Father Christmas, like. I kept thinking to myself, over and over again, they don't have accidents on the ranges, no way! Well they had now, so fuck them! Except they hadn't, because Ken had topped himself. The bastards! Ken had shot himself. The fucking, fucking bastards!

His room was locked, so I couldn't get a drink in there even if he'd left some brandy going spare, and I couldn't go down the Naafi, I was too fucking scruffy, never mind the puffy eyes and snot. My other combats were filthy from the ranges yesterday and the ones I

147

had on had at least two days crap on now, but I couldn't be arsed to clean them for the morning neither. I tore the trousers off and folded them up underneath my mattress, which is the idle bastards' method – leave 'em for the fairies. I put on trackie bottoms and old trainers, and I rubbed the fucking tearstains off my face.

I felt like death, like shit, like bloody murder. I felt like getting blasted, pissed as a total fucking rat. So watch out Catterick. God bloody help you.

Six

The only trouble was, there'd been a slight mistake. The only other trouble was, by the time I found out, it was too late. I walked into the third pub and walked up to the bar, and despite the fact I was streaked with rain and looked a total tramp, they knew I was army so they served me, you don't cut off the pipe that squirts the cash, do you? I only ordered lager anyway. I'd had some double whiskies in the other pubs, tipped into me pints, and they hadn't let me do it last time, so I played it a bit cool. To tell the truth I was so pissed by now, I didn't realise what the problem was when I walked round the pillar and saw Ken sitting there. The problem was that he was dead. I'd sat down with him and said "Cheers mate" before I remembered it. It was quite a bleeding shock.

"Tiny," he said. He slurred the word a bit. His eyes were rolling in his head, like boiled eggs with blood in them. Then they cleared. "Tiny? What's up mate! You look as if you've seen a fucking ghost."

I knocked me pint over, across the table, all across the chairs, all over everywhere. They couldn't see me from the bar, so that was all right. Anyway, it was Catterick. More often it was someone's stomach lining.

"Fucking hell, Ken. Fucking hell, mate."

He'd already made it to his feet. His trouser leg was soaking but he didn't mind. By the time he got back with two big brandies in his hand, I'd got myself together, and my one didn't touch the sides. It went down like a tosser on the Alton Towers flume.

"Thanks, mate. Thanks, Ken. Same again, is it?"

It took me longer to get served. I couldn't make me fingers do the money. When I got back he'd moved to a drier table. His face was back to normal, too. Another lease of life.

"You heard about the kid then," he said, not a question really. "Mate o' yours, were 'e? You seem a bit cut up."

"A mate?" I said. "Who was it, Ken? I don't even know."

"Young kid called Al. Blonde kid, 'bout eighteen. They told him this morning he weren't passing off the square, the only one in his whole intake. Poor fucker couldn't take it. They took the piss. Everyone. You find out who your mates are, don't you – you ain't got none. Your mother never tells you that, does she?"

"He didn't have one, though, did he?" I said. "A proper mum." I tried to think. I tried to beat my brain. "His real name's not Al neither, is it?"

"Not now it ain't," said Ken. "His name now's Rick O'Shea. That's a joke, in case you're too pissed up to notice. I heard it from his sergeant, then three corporals, it's very funny, so they told me. After that I fucked off out of camp, the place is full of fucking ghouls.

It's worse than downtown Baghdad, at least the Muslims hate each other for a reason, it's a religious thing, int it? Sunni, Shia, Allah's lickle children just love to kill each other."

I drank more brandy. Not exactly sipping, but slower than I had before. I couldn't get my head round it. Albino. Beano. Al. What *was* his fucking name? Not passing off the square. Not getting his badge and beret like his mates. More weeks as a crap-hat. Still a trog, and lots more new trogs passing on the conveyor belt. He'd done it 'cause he couldn't take the strain or something. And they called him ricochet, although he didn't fucking miss, and said good fucking riddance.

"Were you on the ranges when it happened? Do you want another drink?"

"Yeah to both," he said. "But he weren't there, were he? His lot were on parade drill for passing out, they'd been marching up and down like clockwork soldiers. I 'spect that's what got to him. Parade drill and marching, only he weren't going nowhere. Why make him do the drill, then? Let me guess – to make him feel a cunt."

I could imagine it. Even with Sarnt Williams not there to beast-in-chief there'd be some other smart-arse buggers. I bet they'd gave him bloody hell.

"But you don't get loaded rifles, do you?" I said. Of course you don't, not for parade drill. So he must have had some knocked-off rounds.

"That drink," said Ken. "I'll have some orange in it this time. I'm getting flavour blur. Go on, shift your idle arse, you nancy-boy."

I thought I'd have orange in as well, or Coke or summat, because I was getting very pissed, and it was getting me down, it was a bleeding habit. Half the squaddies in the army were piss-artists, and half the homeless sleeping on the streets were ex-army, hadn't anybody ever noticed the connection? When it came to it, though, I had the double brandy straight, to feel the smack behind the eyes. Two whole mouthfuls! Luxury! At least old Ken would always pay his corner.

"Still had to clean his weapon, though, didn't he?" he said. "He went back to his room to get his cleaning kit, but he didn't come outside again and no one bleeding noticed. All the others sat in line and spit'n fucking polished, oil, pull-through, joking with the corporals, and crafty Al locked up his door, got out his stash and bunged one up the spout. Bang. Brains everywhere. He didn't even write a note out to his... Oh, you said he didn't have one. Logical."

He paused a bit. We thought a bit. Then he said quietly, "I wonder if any of my kids would think they've got a father. I wonder if I could ever tell them what I've done." He paused a bit more. "My youngest daughter's only six," he said. "Do you know, Tiny, I can't remember what she's called. No, straight up, I've forgot her fucking name. Deborah, that's it, little Deb. Her sister's Donna. She's got two half-sisters as well, off another of the many loving wives. I couldn't tell you *their* names for a thousand fucking pounds. Just for the moment."

It was his turn to get the drinks in, but he'd gone into Stop. That was okay, except I could see his eyes going off, I knew him didn't I, we were old buddies now. I needed something, fast, to cheer him up.

"D'you know what, Ken?" I said. "It could be worse, mate. D'you know I thought it must be you when I heard it on the block. I thought you'd gone apeshit or something. I thought you were the fucking dead-un."

He looked at me and his eyes were sharp and clear, if only for the moment. I thought maybe he was going to take it the wrong way, as if I was getting at him somehow, although I don't know how. Then he shook his head. The bright look went away and he got down again. Down in the dumps.

"I told you, Tiny. Don't you listen? Old soldiers never die, they just fade away." He laughed, although it wasn't much of one. "That was the saying in the old days, did you know that – old soldiers fade away. We don't now though, we slide into the gutter with our Tennants and our Special Brew. It's the kids that top themselves. Except they never do, do they? They have accidents. That's the army's story."

He lifted his glass and seemed surprised to find it empty. He looked at mine, and it was empty too.

"They're prone to accidents, the very young," he said. "They're so prone it's a wonder that they let 'em go and fight at all. It's danger-ous, fighting, I'd refuse if I was you, mate, I'd tell 'em that you've got a cold or something." He paused. "I wouldn't go again, I wouldn't. And that's straight up."

He was going down, but he got to his feet and to the bar. Coming back he didn't spill a drop, although his hands were shaking. The pub was full now, it was getting late. People knew us, from the camp, people knew the both of us, but they never spoke, they never even said hello. There was a black cloud hanging over him, and I was on the inside looking out. It felt like he was drowning. It felt like I was drowning too.

"D'you know what I saw last time in Iraq?" he said, after another silence. "I saw them cut a woman's head off in the street, not chop it off but saw it off, cold blood. We were close enough to see the details, and they did it so we *would* see, because we couldn't open fire, it was in a market, other women all around, and kids, and old geezers and ladies in their robes. Our translator said they said she was a collaborator, she'd been talking to the people on the other side, she was a Sunni but she'd been talking Shite, our little joke, to join in their insanity. It was stunted for our benefit, the translator said, they'd've rather waited for the TV people but they thought they'd never come. They sawed her head off slowly, side to side, and she was groaning and half-talking, squirting blood, and Tiny, you couldn't even throw up because if you took your eye off them some bastard would have plugged you, wouldn't he? Savages, eh? Utter fucking savages. And back in base that night, one of our lads, twenty two or twenty three, normal British soldier, salt of the earth – he started selling pictures of it that he'd taken on his mobile. Tenner a time for copies. Tenner a bleeding time."

For some reason that didn't get to me a lot. I mean, it sounded awful, but then they did this sort of business, didn't they, I just couldn't really get a grip on it no more. My main feeling, honestly, was I was glad I wasn't there, it didn't sound much like a war at all, it sounded like a slaughterhouse. I guessed that that was Ken's point, really. He'd had enough. He'd seen too much of it.

But then he started in on other things, and he got so gruesome that I almost lost my taste for drink. The last time he'd been, he said, before they shipped him off to Germany to "catch up on some sanity," he'd seen the bloody lot – Americans raping little girls, squaddies chucking people into filthy open sewage ditches to teach them how to swim, and worst of all collecting bodies with the Iraqi so-called army, nuts and gangsters and religious loonies to a man, the whole damn lot of them.

"We picked up more bodies than hyenas in brown boots," he said. "Not just dead bodies, but minced, diced, sliced, dismembered. Kids of ten or so with their eyes drilled out with Black and Deckers and their teeth pulled out with pliers. Young girls with their tits cut off. Old men and ladies stabbed up the bum until they bled to death. I'm telling you, Tiny, it were grim. It were fucking diabolical."

He lapsed off into silence. I said "D'you want another drink?" because I couldn't think of anything else to say, but he didn't seem to hear me.

"We went in because someone said they were out to kill us," he said. "We invaded them because of weapons that weren't even there. They said they'd call us saviours, we were bringing peace, and it was a straightforward, stinking lie. I watched Blair say it. I watched him on the telly, and for years and years and years I could not believe that he were lying. I were a soldier, Tiny. I were proud. I were that proud, kid, you would not befucking*lieve* it. A soldier of the fucking *Queen*!"

Even in the throbbing noise, the bass notes and the squaddies shouting at each other in the way of friendly chat, Ken was loud all of a sudden. But it didn't last. He looked into his empty glass, and he held it up then dropped it. It smashed on the table and he ground his hand on it, and he didn't even seem to feel the pain.

"Fifty thousand dead," he said. "A hundred thousand dead, two hundred, three, maybe plenty, plenty more, we don't even fucking know and no way are we fucking saying, are we? That's our gift to them poor bastards, Tiny, us soldiers of the Queen. So what am I now? War criminal? George Dubya said his God told him to go in and save them, our twat said his God would judge him right and turned a Catholic to make it double sure, and the Muslims said theirs would burn us all in hell. I wonder which God's right?"

"Bush loved his," I said, quite drunkenly. "Blair loved both of his, straight and left-footer. Old Saddam loved his too, no bleeding doubt of it, and what about the Taliban? The question is, old mate – I wonder what God fucking thinks of them?"

This struck me as dead funny, and also pretty clever in a way. But there was a crash as Ken's head dropped onto the table, onto the broken glass, and I saw blood leaking everywhere.

Whoops. Time to go. Cheers, mate. I'd like to stay and help you, but I can't. I remembered what he'd said. A soldier of the Queen. He used to be a soldier of the Queen. I can't help you, Ken, I'm sorry mate, I can't. Can anyone?

Death of a Hero

One

I don't think I meant to run, it's just one of those things that happen, innit? My only feeling when I staggered out into the street
was to get away from Ken. I wouldn't even know why to that, if you
asked me. Okay, he was pissed and bleeding and collapsed, but it
was maybe all his stories that had got to me, and where it went from
there. Ken was mental, and Al Beano had just topped himself. The
best Ken could hope for was a medical discharge – depression, the
magic word! – and the worst, if he didn't stop shooting his mouth
off, was dishonourable, even jail. If the ginger bastard really was an
undercover man, if Goughie tried to brown-nose by ratting on his
oppos… Well, shit.

Al Beano. I still couldn't remember his real name, but I'd never call
him Rick O'Shea, no way. I thought I'd better go to Tesco's and
get some brandy for the trip. The trip? What trip? I'd bought the
bloody stuff, opened the bloody bottle, and took a giant swig outside
on the pavement before that filtered through my bonce. What trip?

It was like when I found out about Bridgie and all the Irish bastards,
in a way. I can remember how I felt then, and the only word I can
bring up to describe it is "confused." She didn't like me maybe,
but we were meant to be together, weren't we? I mean, we slept
together, and she took all my cash, and then I found out she was
fucking my new mates, and she didn't even mind when I found

out! I mean, what was that all about? Explain it to me, someone.
Explain the deal.

By the time I got to the station in Darlington I was arseholed, no
doubt of that at all, I didn't even know how I'd bloody got there, although a taxi would be my best guess. But I was arseholed, and I sat
on a bench looking at the ticket I'd just bought and wondering what
the fucking fuck. Why the fuck I'd bought one to Newcastle, when
I'd never been and didn't want to go. Why the fuck I'd bought one
anyway. What was I doing? Was I on the run? And if so – why? I
sat there blinking for a while or two (maybe a minute, maybe half
an hour, I really do not know) and nothing came to mind. Slurps of
brandy, that was nice. I was cold and wet and muzzy, but the brandy
warmed me up.

Where was I going? Why Newcastle? Ah – that came back. I had
been going to Manchester, to go and see my old mate Shofiq. No,
not Shahid, Shofiq, another one, I'm a Paki-lover remember and my
name's Hassan, although I don't go there very often, not even on me
own, and I'd missed the train. Shofiq would've put me up, he lived
in Withington and he was a total pisshead and all right. I got my
mobiles off him, and he might even have a car by now. He'd hide
me up, or drive me off somewhere, maybe back to Blackburn for a
while, to see me mum. She'd be pleased I'd left the army. Pleased?
She'd be out of her mind! *Now* how would I earn a fucking living?
And I hadn't left, I'd done a runner, too!

I felt terrible, then. No, terrified. Hollowed out with panic, gal-
loping bleeding fear. What would they do to me? Would I go to
prison? Would they send out RMPs to jam me into handcuffs?
Would they beat me up? We were always talking about it, everybody

did now and again, but I'd never known a squaddie who'd took the
plunge and run. When the ticket woman said I'd missed the train
to Manchester I'd felt relieved. Back at camp they'd have guessed
I'd gone there, wouldn't they, the heart of Lancashire, the northern
Mecca? But Newcastle? They'd never, ever think of that. And then
I saw the coppers, and I froze.

They were only wandering, I think, but when they clocked me it
gave their lives a purpose, you could tell. They strolled towards me,
both big and fattish, both steaming in the damp, and not unfriendly,
not at all, not threatening. They knew I was a squaddie, though, for
some reason people always do, which is another bleeding mystery
– we don't even have squaddie haircuts any more. I tried to hide
the bottle by my legs. I didn't have a bag or anything. I didn't even
have a coat.

"'Allo, mate, you look wet enough. What you doing?"

I looked up and give a smile.

"I'm off to Newcastle. I've got me ticket. I'm going to see me
girlfriend."

"We know you've got your ticket," said the other one. "You wanted
to go to Manchester. Moved, has she? That was sudden."

Smartarse. I couldn't think of anything to say.

"You on the run, are you? Want us to take you back to Catterick?
We've got a nice warm car outside."

159

"I'm not on the run. I'm just..."

I ran out of words. So much for them not knowing, just having a little wander, like. Of course they fucking knew. They even knew my fucking name.

"Private Hassan. Andrew. Back at camp, they reckon that you..."

But the train was pulling in. Newcastle. Noisy bastard. The copper stopped the talking for a while. He looked at his watch, then double-checked it with the station clock. I stood up. I picked up my bottle. No point in trying to hide it, anyway. The PA started waffling. I didn't listen.

"He's got another half an hour yet," the other copper said. He said to me: "You've got another half an hour, Andy. Before they mark you down official. You going back?"

I couldn't believe this. Maybe I was dreaming it. I felt pissed enough.

"Can I go now?" I said. "I've got to catch me train."

It would be leaving in a second. There were fuck-all people getting on and off. The copper nodded.

"We can't stop you, mate."

"We can only give advice."

"For half an hour. Then you're official. AWOL, on the run."

"We can give you some advice, though."

"Thanks," I said. I didn't even say fuck off. I tried a smile, but my features weren't having any. I felt terrible. I felt as if I was going to die, just drop to pieces on the platform. One of them was on his radio as the train door closed behind me.

It was raining worse in Newcastle, and I was more than half expecting the police or RMPs would be there to meet me. More than half hoping as well, I think, although I'm sure I wasn't sure. By the time I got to Newcastle I'd be officially absent, and if they didn't take me back, what then? I was in trouble, in deeper trouble, but I didn't know how deep, I didn't have a bleeding clue. I guessed the longer I was out the worse though, that was logical. So if I was going to be arrested, surely the sooner the better? And they knew where I was. They had to, didn't they? They had to pick me up.

But they didn't. I stood about and looked all over, and there wan't a uniform in sight, except the railway lot. It was pretty late, and the weather was terrible, though the air was pretty warm. I was pissed as arseholes, I'd left the empty bottle on the train, and I wanted to lie down and sleep, or maybe vomit. I was lost on this great big giant station, in a dump I'd only ever heard of, and I didn't know what to do, I didn't have a fucking *prayer*. I rang up Shahid.

"Tiny! You bastard! You could've caught me on the job!"

Some chance with Shahid, I'd never known him at that sort of thing. But I couldn't joke. There wasn't any humour to come out of me.

"Mate. Sha. I need your help, mate. I'm in the shit."

There was music in the background, and laughs, and pool balls. I must've said "are you in a pub," or something, although I don't remember that I did.

"Yeah," he said. "That dump we went in on that first night out – no lager. It's not so bad though when there's no one in it, which there ain't when they've moved on to town. Just me and Ashton and a few other lads, it's a sort of lock-in. What's up?"

"I've quit," I said. "I've gone AWOL, I've done a runner. I'm stuck up in Newcastle in the rain."

"What you done that for, you daft twat?" he said. "Newcastle? Poor bastard. You'll go to fucking prison, mate. What's happened?"

"Nothing," I said. "Nowt. Nowt special. A kid got shot at camp. Topped himself, but..."

"Did you know him?"

"Nah. Just a crap-hat. But..."

"Tiny, what's it got to do with you, mate? You can't do it, Tiny! You can't just do a runner. You'll get... they'll throw the book at you!"

"I can't take it, Sha. I'm pissed off. You know we've talked about it. I'm getting out."

"You can't get out! Not by going AWOL! Shit, it's not that bad, we have some good times, don't we? We'll be back up soon, me and Ashton will, the Three Must-get-fucking-beers! England needs us, mate, to fight the savages! We're the Great White Bleeding Hope!"

He was trying hard to get me out of it, but that didn't even raise a smile. It *nearly* did – I had a vision of the Great White Hope, one drunk, one black, one Paki – but the gloom crushed down again. I was in a city street, well after midnight, in the fucking pissing rain.

"Look," I said. "Stop talking bollocks, Sha. I need somewhere to sleep. Tell me where to sleep."

There was a long pause after this, and I thought he'd hung up, even, until I realised I could still hear music and so on. My head was banging now. Clattering. When he came back on his voice was really serious, no more stupid jokes.

"Look," he said. "Tiny. Mate. We've talked about it, yeah? The army's just a prison sentence, man, but not so bad, except the food. We've got to stick it out, we've got to fight the lunatics. Look, mate – this is what to do. Phone Catterick. Phone the camp. Tell 'em where you are and what you've done. Tell them you're coming back. You've got to, Tiny. You've fucking *got* to. Okay?"

No, not okay. Not okay at all. No way okay.

"Not going back. I need somewhere to sleep, Sha, that's all. If you ain't got no suggestions, fair enough. No way I'm going back, Shahid. No fucking way."

He put Ashton on. At last, I thought – some sense. That's how pissed I was. Some sense from Ashton. Jesus.

"Well ain't you the bright boy," he said. He didn't even do a silly voice. "Look, old mate, he's right, you've got to fucking listen. Go back before you're absolutely fucked. D'you want to spend the next four years inside? D'you want to end up down in Colchester? D'you ever want to see the light of day again?"

"Oh piss off, Ashton. I've had enough of fucking bullshit. I ain't going back. I've had it, mate. I've had it up to *here*."

I could hear him breathing down the phone. That and pub noise in the background. I was jealous. I was lonely, too.

"You will have, mate," he said. His voice was mild, he was really trying to be calm and sober. "Look, you've got to pull yourself together, Ti, you're in the shit already, ain't you? Have you got a pencil on you, a pen or something? All right then, I've got some mates. They know I've got a soft spot for white trash, so I expect they'll let you in okay unless they're all unconscious in their pits. I'll try and ring 'em, anyway, and – oh hang about, Sha wants another word. He's nicked my mobile, cheeky bastard. He's been ringing camp."

I couldn't believe it. I had a bit of paper in my hand and I fucking near fell over. "You what!" I shrieked. "You fucking bastard, Sha! What you fucking *doing*?"

"Calm down, Cynthia, I ain't doing nothing, as it happens. I've been on directory to find the camp at Catterick, and I've got fucking nowhere, it don't exist, apparently. Bloke give me a central number in the end, down London somewhere, and guess what – no reply! He said I wouldn't get one. He said the army only answers during working hours, it's a well-known fact. He seemed to think I should've had a special number, seeing I'm a soldier. That's fucking likely, innit?"

"Good if we've been invaded, eh?" said Ashton, in the background. "Give us the phone, Sha. Tiny. Write down this address. Just for tonight, right, and I'll ring you in the morning, yeah? You're fucking *going back*."

Half an hour later I was standing on the pavement in the rain outside this little terraced house, and the only nearby sound was the taxi disappearing down this long, long road. I knocked again, and listened. Unconscious in their pits – what had he meant by that? No lights, no action, nobody. I knocked again. And knocked again. What had he bloody meant by that?

Oh you bastard, Ash, I told myself, five minutes later. Some sort of rotten joke this is, you bastard, not funny to an enemy, let alone a mate, not fucking *funny*. I knocked again. I knocked harder. I kicked seven kinds of shit out of the door. And at last a light came on. Footsteps. Like something in a bleeding horror film.

Whoops, I thought. I heard a chain rattling on the door. Whoops, I'm going to get my head smacked up for this, I've bloody nearly kicked the bastard in. It'll be a big black hairy bruiser. It'll be a giant. Poor little me. I giggled. I was pissed unconscious. I tittered like a total tit.

I didn't think I'd even feel a thing.

Two

Black, yes, but not a bruiser, no way a bruiser, not even after nine-ty seven pints. She was small in fact, but *really* small, about half my size, as far as I could see. She was in a nightie, and she looked more than half asleep. She just stared at me, through the gap. Not stupid, then. That chain had rattled going on, not coming off.

"Hi. I'm... well, I'm... Well Ashton rung you, yeah?"

"Ashton? *Ashton?* No, did 'e 'eck." There was Manchester in her voice, unmistakable, and I thought thank God, thank God for that. Don't take a lot, does it, when you're pissed? "The phone's knack-ered," she added, like an afterthought. "We an't bothered, really, we use us mobiles, don't we? What, you an army mate, are you? Why aye, man-pet – you're soaking to the skin."

She said that in a different sort of accent (Geordie – like them wankers on the box, that Ant and Dec), and it was a kind of joke, to make me feel okay. Then she smiled this big wide smile and rattled the chain off, and said "D'you want a brew? I'm called Carole, with an E." Oh, it was like bloody coming home.

It started slowly, because basically, I didn't have a thing to say. I felt so, like, you know, embarrassed, out of place, that I sat there like a total dick for ages. What I really wanted was a piss, it was getting desperate, but you don't like to say, do you, specially not to a girl. All she wanted to do was make me feel at home I think, so she give it the small talk for a while and it got worse and worse. I mean, she didn't know me, I didn't know her, and I'd turned up in the middle of the night, well pissed. What *should* we've talked about? The price of fish in Grimsby?

In the end I think I was going to literally piss myself, and I couldn't even stand up now because my dick was swole up like a firehose and she would've thought – well, God knows what she would have thought, but she'd have been dead wrong, whatever. And I think I might've made a little noise, I might've had a little moan or something, or maybe she was psychic, because she suddenly bounced up to her feet and sort of shouted.

"Oh my God, that brew! Oh look I'm sorry, love. Do you take sugar? Oh God, what a cow!"

She shot off to the kitchen then, and I shot off down the passage to the pisser, and nearly had to break me thing in half to get it out. Wall, seat, cistern, they all got a squirt before I could control it, but I used plenty of paper to mop up with so I hope she never noticed. I had her figured for a nurse in any case, so I spose she wouldn't've minded all that much.

She offered food with the mug of Typhoo ("only cheese and bread and stuff like that, sorry.") but I think I would have chucked up on the spot so that was easy. But then she offered paracetamol and I had a go at that, and, being stupid, I asked her if she had some weed, which I did not want and didn't even know why I'd mentioned it. She knew, though. She laughed.

"Bog off," she said. "If you was a racist Ash wouldn't bother with you so no stupid jokes to break the ice, okay? You don't want weed, and I ain't got none, end of story. And no more booze, okay? You've took your paracetamol."

So she was a nurse then. I was blushing. I felt a total prat.

"Sorry," I said. Well, sort of mumbled. "It's just I'm…I'm…"

"Half pissed. Yeah, I know, love. But you're here now, you're all right. We've got a bed for you and you can sleep it off all day tomorrow if you want to, I'll be off to work and the others are away, and you're more than welcome, anytime. What you doing here, are you on leave or something? Funny place to spend it, Newcastle, if you don't mind me saying so."

I've got a way with words, you might have worked it out by now – I can't express meself even when I know roughly what I'm thinking. Now, today, this moment, I didn't have the foggiest idea, to be quite honest, or maybe I did – the foggiest, that's what it felt like, inside my head. Thick fog. Confusion. A little bit of pain.

"I'm on the run," I said. "I've quit. I've just fucked off. Sorry."

"Oh," she said. "I don't know what to say. 'That's nice' don't seem to cover it, somehow. Oh bloody 'ell, love. You poor thing. Do you want another cup of tea?"

That made us both laugh, because I'd hardly started on the first one, but I bloody did, an' all. I chucked it down my neck and held the

mug out and she took it and went out, a swish of long white night-
dress. I sat down and pulled myself together. I sat down and wiped
my fucking eyes. When she came back she gave me tea, then turned
an electric fire on. She sat down in an easy chair and tucked her
legs up under her. Shit, I thought. She thinks it's going to be a long
night. She thinks I'm going to talk. She's going to die of fucking
boredom.

She didn't mention me being on a runner, that was the funny thing.
She asked me where I came from, and how I knew Ashton, and
who our other mates were, and what was Blackburn like, was it a
dump like everybody said, but nothing to do with bunking off, not
even why I'd ended up in Newcastle like a drownded rat. When I
got tongue-tied she didn't laugh, and if I stopped talking halfway
through a sentence she didn't hurry me, she didn't seem to mind at
all, or even notice. She made me endless brews, and some time later
I got a tin of soup and bread, then three square corner yoghurts,
bloody A. Before I really knew it we'd sat up half the night and she
was bloody great to me, she was like a sister, the best a bloke could
ever have, and I was getting sober – without pain!

There were four of them shared the flat, it turned out – all girls
– and one of them was Ashton's ex, and he still kept in touch and
came to see them sometimes. I must've raised me eyebrows or
summat, because she said "to *see*, I said, and nothing else. They're
friends, okay?" and I bloody believed her, which put old Ashton in a
brand new light, no danger! The way she said it, I wondered if she
was a schoolteacher, not a nurse, but she just worked in an office,
that's all, in a supermarket. She said Ashton was a great bloke, and
he was engaged to his ex's sort of cousin, and he was like a little

lamb. Jesus, I thought. Where do we go from there? Next Shahid'll be a bleeding Catholic.

The girls were at a concert somewhere – Whitstable or Whitehaven Bay or some other place I'd never heard of – so I had a choice of beds, she said, not just Ashton's sofa in the telly room. I didn't even *wonder* if she'd let me kip with her, I didn't even think about it. She was just there, all kind and sisterly, in this big white nightie, and she was smiling, like tea and sympathy, big style. And when she finally did get round to asking why I'd run, it seemed completely natural, like she really wanted to know, not just looking for a bit of dirt or scandal. I was still tongue-tied, though, but only 'cause I'd never put it into words before, not even to myself. Why *had* I? Why had I just walked through the gates last night without signing out when I'd thought that Ken was dead, why had I give the duty squaddie the big finger when he called out to me? Why?

I said: "Carole, no bullshit. But I'm fucked if I know – oh, sorry, like. Is it all right to swear?"

"It hasn't stopped you so far, Andy," she said, laughing. "Don't mind me, love, I'd join in if I could, like. Way I were brought up, know what I mean?"

The Andy shook me. I must have told her my real name. Politeness city, eh? Or the booze, who knows? I was almost stone-cold now, though. Just the start-off of a splitting headache.

"I don't know, though, and that's God's honest truth," I said. "I mean – it's shit, that's all, the whole thing's shit. No rhyme or reason to it. The officers are stupid, they try to be your mates and call you by your nickname once a fortnight, and they get it wrong."

You could see her thinking, fucksake, is that *all?* And it wasn't, of course, but how to say it?

"That sounds pretty…well," she said. "Well, I mean…"

"Look, I can't tell you, Carole, that's the honest truth. I mean, well, fuck, that's just the officers, innit, and… Look, the sergeants. I mean. Well, one of 'em's right into me at the moment, he's a total bastard, Williams he's called. Him and his mates. And he beasts the corporals, too, and the lancejacks. Thrashes them. You know? They're scared of him, terrified, know what I mean?"

She didn't, you could see it. Beasts, thrashes, it was double-Dutch to her. I struggled to explain, to find the words, and then I couldn't. I played the easy card, I went a different route. Look on the positive, as mum would say. Look on the pissing positive.

"At least it isn't boring, though," I said. "Say what else about Sarnt Williams, he isn't boring. The army is, though. Maybe that's why I run, who knows? That's the worst thing, Carole, that's the thing that gets down in your bones. It's so fucking, *fucking* boring. Same thing, day after day, day after fucking day. It never changes."

"Tell me about it," she said. "I work in a supermarket." But she didn't say it in a piss-off way, it was just a thing to say, part of the conversation. She was interested, still. She was on my side, all the bleeding way. She said: "Why did you join up, though? If it's so boring? Or didn't they mention that in the Army Offices?"

171

We had another little laugh at that, she was dead smart, Carole. And I heard meself tell her the truth, say things I don't think I really knew myself. About how I'd gone to uni because my mother thought I ought to try, to "have the chance," although I really knew I didn't want to do it, because I couldn't really see the point. Fact was I only knew at my age people were meant to be growing up, and I didn't think I'd even started. Being out there, earning a living, relationships and children – it was a thousand miles away. I figured it would come to me, or I would come to it, but it wasn't yet, the process wasn't even starting, stirring, rearing its ugly fucking head.

"I was studying," I said. "They called it studying. A subject I was sort of guided into, that I'd never thought of before and I've never thought of since. It was a big black hole. I was diving in to show I was maturing, to make my mother proud, to say thank you for all she'd tried to do. Oh shit."

"And?"

"I failed. By the end of my first year, I failed every subject, every exam. I didn't know what I was doing, I didn't know why I was doing it, I just wanted it to end. I felt terrible. I felt a complete and utter failure."

"But you had the A-levels!" Carole said. "You're not thick, you passed them! Did you take resits?"

I shrugged.

"I'd rather've cut my throat, quite honestly. You say that I'm not thick, but that's the way it felt, I'm telling you. And all me old mum's hopes. And all the cash I'd cost her. I felt like bloody crying, honestly."

She looked at me.

"Hard man." She grinned. "But your mum did, didn't she?"

Smart bitch you are, I thought. But I really like you, Caz, I really do.

"She did when I joined the army. Floods of it. Lake Niagara."

"Yeah," said Carole. "I should bloody think so too. Why did you do it, though? Bit different from university. D'you want another brew?"

She yawned, as if her brain was going on to automatic, and I yawned too. Time for bed soon. Jesus, I was tired. Jesus bleeding H. But I thought about her question. Bit different. Yeah.

"It seemed a good idea," I said. "No brains needed, no school-type bollocks, no eff-all."

And money in the bank, and no one to feed and worry for me day to day, and someone to tell me what to do. I did it to take the pressure of my mum, that's how daft I was. At that age war and life and death meant nothing to me. It never occurred how much they'd mean to mum.

"You men are mental," Carole said. "You just don't get it do you, Ashton's just the same. We worry for him. We worry for him all the time."

Ashton again. I couldn't get my head round it, quite honestly.

"It wasn't just me," I said, defensively. "My sister Vronnie talked her round as well. She said statistically I had much more chance of being run down by a bus in town than stopping a bullet, and at least I'd end up learning something useful – like a brickie, say, or a plumber or mechanic. Much more useful than I'd learn at uni, anyway."

"And did you?"

"Did I fuck as like, it was a con like every other bleeding thing they said was going to happen. I learned piss-artistry that's all, and Olympic standard swearing, and a bit of minor thieving, and I go mad with rage if someone crosses me, and I earn fuck all and owe a bleeding fortune. I even owe the government me one-year student loan back. The only good thing is, in the army, I'll never earn enough to have to pay it! They can bloody whistle."

I wanted a drink again. Not tea. I nearly asked for one. Carole unfolded her legs and leaned towards me. Her sleepiness had gone away.

"So did you hate it straight away, then? When did you realise you'd got it wrong?"

I thought a bit, but I didn't need to think for long. They pitch it brilliant – it's quite good, it's interesting, until it's just too late to walk away. I think I realised it about five weeks after I'd missed me chance to go. After I'd signed up for four years.

"Well," I said. "I didn't hate it from the start, to be quite honest I sort of loved it. I mean, I got fit, I lost a ton of weight, then put it back in muscle, I played with rifles, played lots of sport, drove Land Rovers off road, all sorts of boss things. It was like...well, it was sort of like I'd found what I was looking for, my mum was chuffed to death. Still worried, like, but chuffed as well. 'He's loving it,' she used to tell the aunties. 'New lease of life, I think he's found his fucking feet at last.' Not fucking, obviously, this was me mum, but you know what I mean. When it changed, I didn't dare to tell her, I didn't want to, it was so nice to have done something right at last. I haven't even told her yet how bone it got, how utter, utter crap. She hasn't even got a clue."

I thought that through, as well. Not completely true, but not so far off.

"I did say once I wan't so keen," I said. "When I'd finished training. There's a lot of bullying and racism when you join an actual regiment and I did get pissed one night and say I hated it. But she went mad, really. Well, it was more she looked as if I'd hit her in the face. Terrible."

"Oh God," said Carole.

"Yeah. She went 'But you said you loved it! Oh love, it seemed so wonderful!' And me sister's like 'But it's money coming in! It's only for four years!' Yeah. Four years unless they shoot me brains out, I thought, that used to be her fucking worry once, that didn't last long, did it? And then mum goes: 'But what about Bridgie? Won't she be disappointed?' and I bloody near threw up. Talk about clutching at fucking straws!"

"Bridgie? Is that your girlfriend?"

"Sort of. Well, used to be. The thing is, they both hated her. She was Irish. Well, she was a royal pain, in actual fact. But they were prepared to like her again, pretend to, anyway – just to keep me in. Keep me out of mum's hair, like. Jesus. Bloody diabolical."

"But you were going to go to war," she said. "Afghanistan or something, they must've known that, surely? I mean, what if you'd been killed?"

"Yeah," I said. "Maybe they really hoped I'd die, d'you reckon? Deep down. Save a lot of bleeding bother."

Carole's face went furious.

"That's bollocks, Andy! I'm not having that, no way! You don't mean that, do you? That's just ruddy crap."

It could have been a shouting match. I couldn't let that happen. And she was bloody right.

"Okay, okay," I said, "I'll take that back, okay? Maybe I'm just shit scared is all. Maybe I'm just a coward. Am I allowed to say that? Does that sound right?"

"Well, I don't know, do I?" she said, still pretty brisk. "Are you? Scared, I mean?" Her voice went softer. "If you aren't you ruddy ought to be, it don't make you a coward in my book. It's dangerous. Lots of lads get killed. It's terrible. I'm sorry if I shouted, love. I didn't mean it, either."

I shook me head. I was being serious.

"Yeah, I guess I might be, in the end," I said. "There's more chance with a bleeding bus, though, when you think about it, int there? It's not the war I'm scared of, it's the army. It's the shit. The bollocks. The way we just exist to save some bugger's skin. Some shitty politician's skin who started it, like. We may not even get to war it's turning into shit so fast. The whole thing's so fucked up I wouldn't be surprised. A glitch. Computer error."

She smiled, but she wan't that daft, no way. She shook her head and let out a big sigh.

"That's not what Ashton says," she said. "He reckons you're going pretty soon, he says it's on the cards. Afghanistan, Helmand, whatever. He says the story's out."

"The story's always out," I said. "Three times a week it's going to happen, something, anything. It never bleeding does. The only thing you know for sure is you know damn all, and the damn all that you know is definite. That's how they like it."

"Well he's getting married, though," said Carole. "That's how sure Ashton is. Didn't you know that? He's got a honeymoon booked in a few weeks. Pre-wedding honeymoon. Malta or somewhere. Majorca maybe."

First I'd heard about a honeymoon, but it sounded right for Ash. If he did get posted and he missed the actual wedding, fair enough. But he'd get the honeymoon in, no bleeding way! I grinned, a bit sickly. To be honest, I didn't care no longer. Suddenly, I wanted me bed. Suddenly, I thought I might fall over soon. I was completely buggered.

I sort of half stood up, and Carole got up, too. Her face was full of sympathy. She shook her head.

"God, you look terrible," she said. "I'll wake you in the morning, shall I? Before I go to work. Look, you can stay here longer if you like, you're more than welcome, honest, love." She stopped. "But I'd go back if I was you. I really, really would."

I looked at her. What did she know? She looked straight back, and give a little smile.

"Why?" I said.

"Because," she said. "Well, I don't really know. It just feels right, know what I mean? You've only missed a day, they won't do much, will they? Anyone can tell that you was drunk. I'll be a witness if you like. I'll give you my mobile number. Tell 'em to ring me. I don't mind, Andy. I think you ought to go."

"Hah!" I said. I was going to slur my words. "You just want to see me get blown up, don't you! You just want to see me in Afghanistan!"

She didn't smile, but she wasn't angry, neither. She just looked at me.

"You're not afraid of that, I know you're not," she said. "And your mates are going. Think how bored you'll be without them. Now that's *really* boring. Go on to bed. In there. D'you want another brew?"

"I'll piss myself," I said. Last gasp of bravado.

"You won't be the first one," she said. "Sadie was the last. On her birthday, silly cow. You get to bed. I'll leave the light on in the loo."

She walked across and kissed me. I thought that I might cry. It was terrible.

"I'm called Tiny," I said. "Not Andy. Thanks."

"Size don't matter," she said, and laughed like a drain. "Go and get your head down, love. I'd like to hear the rest, one day, all the ins and outs. But go back in the meantime, Tiny. Do it for me. Do it for yourself. Okay? Night-night."

And she went out through the door.

Three

Shahid rung up in the morning, and he'd already rung the camp, the crazy bastard. He'd told the switchboard he was my dad and told them to pass a message on. That he'd spoke to me, and I was in Newcastle, and I was coming back to camp and I'd got pissed but okay now. I couldn't believe it, really. That he'd had the bloody neck. But Carole had gone to work so I couldn't talk to her, and when I rung up Sha again to argue he told me he was busy, and piss off back to Catterick. So I did.

It was like some sort of nasty dream, going in. The squaddie on the gate looked me up and down and asked me if I'd slept in a pigsty or a hedge, then laughed his socks off and said I had to report to the RSM immediate and he was fucking glad he wan't in my shoes. The corporal in the RSM's office told me to go and have a wash and change into a uniform, and come back in fifteen minutes, and God help me if I wasn't super-smart. And when I looked for my trousers they were underneath my mattress, no cleaner than the night before. I got back looking like a victim of a bomb blast, and the RSM didn't bollock me at all, he even smiled.

"Jesus, Hassan," he said. "What a mess. I hope your story's good, lad. Your father's on your side, apparently. He rang up, did you know? Explained it to the switch."

I swallowed.

"Thank you, sir," I said. (He was the RSM. The NCO you did call sir). "He's... he's good, my dad. He told me to come back. He said it was the best."

Jesus. Now Shahid was my father. Official. What would me mother say?

"Aye, well he's dead right there. Go in now. Captain's waiting. You'd better tell him you fell off an elephant or something. It could explain the way you look."

I was starting sweating. This was all wrong, everyone was being nice. I knew the Captain would be if the Sarnt Major was, because the Captain was as soft as shit. He was sitting when I opened the door, looking at his keyboard. He glanced up and smiled.

"Give me a minute, Private. Take a seat. Nice of you to press your uniform. Sorry – joke."

Jesus. He was trying to put me at my ease. Jesus. I could easy shit myself. Then he turned away from the screen, and he said: "Well."

I swallowed.

"Er. Yessir. Sorry, sir. I mean I'm... I'm sorry, sir. I mean it. Sir."

His eyes were pretty keen in fact, they were sort of boring into me. The trouble was I wasn't sorry at all, it was a lie. I wondered if he knew, but I didn't really care, I just hoped I didn't get the glasshouse. I wished I'd stayed away. Gone on the run. Got a full-time job. Say McDonald's. Oh bleeding hell. Alternative career. Oh bleeding, bleeding hell.

"Why did you do it, Tiny? Do you know?"

Tiny! That really put the fears up me. Was I here to get a medal? I licked my lips. Mouth like shit, despite the toothbrush job I'd done. Made me gums bleed.

"Do what, sir?"

Oh shit, bad mistake. I saw his face change.

"I'm sorry, sir," I said. "I didn't mean that, sir, I'm... like, confused. I don't know, sir. That's the honest answer. Sir. I think, sir."

"Are you worried about Afghanistan? There's no certainty we're going there, you know. Nothing's decided yet. It could be Canada, or Germany, or Kosovo."

Now *he* was bullshitting, so that made two of us. But I didn't mind.

"No, sir!" I made it sound like I was annoyed he thought I was a coward. "I'm not a coward, sir. I didn't join the army to run away!" Whoops. But he didn't smile.

"Well, I'm glad to hear that. Just because things out there haven't gone…well, exactly the way the politicos expected, in some people's opinion. Which is nothing to do with us, of course, in any way. We're paid to fight, however hard it might turn out to be. We're soldiers. It's what we do."

To me, he sounded a bit uncomfortable, sort of stilted, but I guess I'll never know what officers really think, or if they even think at all. Squaddies are paid to "fight not think" is fair enough, and officers get paid more than us because they've got a lot more thinking not to do. Or something. My brain was hurting. Cut down the argument. They're a gang of wankers, overpaid.

"Yes, sir," I said. "I won't do it again, sir, honestly. I think it was the drink."

He looked at his computer screen. He tapped the keyboard. He nodded, like a bleeding judge.

"It has been noticed," he said. "Are you worried about your drinking, Tiny? Do you think you ought to talk to the MO?"

Yeah, bloody likely – not. I bet he was a pisshead anyway. My doctor back at home is. Famous for it. I shook my head.

"I don't think that's the problem, sir. I'm maybe a bit... you know, sir. Just at the minute. I got bounced back from the exercises, sir. Me mates are all still there. But I'll cut down. I promise, sir. I'll just stick to beer."

He smiled.

"Very wise. Whisky is the devil, Hassan, that's what they brought me up to think." He read the screen some more. "Hhm. Hhm. Well, you must admit you brought it on yourself. Why did you hit that young police officer? A woman, too, in actual fact. Which makes it rather worse, doesn't it?"

I looked at his soft face and I didn't know if I should hate him or some bugger else. Should I deny it? Was there any point?

"It wasn't me, sir," I said, "and that's the honest truth. It was a sort of riot, that's all I can say. I think someone must have... made a mistake, like. It wasn't me. Sir."

"Hhm," he went. "Oh well. But you're not depressed about it? Not that I'm saying I believe... but you're not claiming...ah... depression?"

The magic word.

"No, sir. I was pissed, sir. Sorry, sir, drunk, sir. I was drunk, not dep— Not suffering from depression, sir. Sir – does it mention Khan on there, sir? Shahid Khan? 'Cause if it says he's a terrorist, I... well he's..."

He was staring at me. Then at the screen, as if to check.

"Shahid Khan? A terrorist? Whyever should it, Private? What are you suggesting? Are you saying that he *is*?"

"No, sir! No, sir! No! No he's *not* sir, that's the point! He hates them, sir, he thinks they're fucking mad! I'm sorry, sir, I—"

"Oh forget it, soldier, swear if you must, for God's sake! Just what is it you're trying to tell me? Just spit it out!"

Christ, this was all completely wrong. I'd kill that Goughie. I'd fucking *kill* him. I was panting, so I took a breath or two. Calmed down.

"I'm sorry, sir. I thought... no, nothing, sir. Private Khan's not a terrorist, sir, he's one of the good guys. He's not even a Muslim any more, he thinks it's mental, sir, he thinks we've got to win."

"Do they bully him? Is that what you're saying, Hassan? Is it a racist thing?"

I was goggling. What *was* this wazzock on about?

"Sir? What, bully Sha? Not likely, sir. No way!"

"Hhm," he went again. I think he was completely lost. He picked up a pen and dropped it back on to the desk.

"No racism, eh? Well, that doesn't surprise me, actually. This is the best outfit I've ever known on the racism front. And bullying, as well. Some regiments are... well, it can be a problem, but... well, I'm glad you agree, Tiny. I'm very proud of it, in actual fact. I'm very proud indeed."

I'd've mentioned Al Beano if I'd had the guts. Or if I'd known his proper fucking name. I had a sudden picture of Johnnie Gough running bollock-naked between two long lines of us on the block in Week Four of our basic training, being punched and kicked and spat at because the corporals said unless we give him some hammer for his messy bed we'd get much worse. And it suddenly got to me. No racism! No bullying! Was he completely fucking *mad?*

"Well!" I said. And I was almost spluttering. "Well the reason they don't bully Shahid, sir – is because he'd bloody kill them! But racism, sir! Well! It's terrible! Black lads and Pakis, sir – they get it in the neck, sir! One lad called Jamal, sir – he quit, don't you remember? They made his life a misery! He damn near fucking topped himself!"

"Watch your language, will you!" said the captain, sharply, and I must've goggled like a fish, because he added: "I will not hear racist insults, understand? It's no help at all to call our Pakistani soldiers names. They are your comrades. They are your friends."

"But…" I went. "But, but… Sir, it's not me that's racist, *they* are! The sergeants! Corporals! Lancejacks! There's even *officers*—"

I thought he'd blow a fuse. He slammed his hand down on his table and his keyboard jumped up in the air. He shouted at me.

"Enough! I do not want to hear this!"

"And bullying!" I said. "I'm bloody sick of it! Take Johnnie Gough!"

My voice was trembling. I was running out of steam. His eyes were
beady on me, but he could see I'd given in. He could see what I was
thinking – *shit, I'm in the shit, big style.* As I wound down I could see
that he'd relaxed. Game set and match to him. He smiled at me, the
patronising twat.

"I think it's the army that you're sick of, Tiny, that's the truth now,
isn't it? You mention Johnnie Gough, for instance, and let me tell you
this – for Private Gough we predict great things, he'll be a credit to the
British Army. I'm right, aren't I? You're just brassed off with things?
Jealous perhaps, just a little teenie weenie bit? Or maybe you're in
love. Is it woman trouble? We can be very sympathetic if you try us."

I shook my head. What could I do? Jealous of fucking Gough. In
love. God bloody save us all.

"No, sir. No, sir. Honestly."

"Listen," he said. "My guess is you've got the jitters, lad, whatever you
might say, and it's nothing to be ashamed of, I do assure you. But I've
told you, and you have my word on it, we are not going to Afghanistan
in the near future, nor Kosovo. You can count on it, you can tell your
friends. Okay? Does that feel better?"

"Sir," I said. I just wanted one more try. I'd spat it out to Carole, I
knew it could be done. "Sir," I said, "I ain't afraid sir, honestly. It's
just that… Oh, I dunno. It's not how I expected, sir, it feels a…it feels
like it's a *waste.* I mean, sir. I'm not stupid, I was told that I could get
a trade, something for *afterwards.* I mean, this lot's not going to last
for ever, is it? Not even that much longer, a lot of people say. I was
promised at the recruitment office, that's why I joined. A bricklayer, a

plumber, you know? And when I started here they knocked me back. They laughed at me."

He was looking at his screen. He was scrolling through and stopping. Then scrolling through again.

"Well the problem is, Hassan," he said. "We don't *need* bricklayers, do we? And anyway, what good's a trowel when some Taliban comes at you in Kandahar? What good's a hod against an IED?"

A grin spread on his face, then he clocked mine and stopped it. We stared at each other, and his mouth went back to normal.

"The point is," he said, "you didn't go to the recruiting office to become a plumber, did you, you went to serve your country. There's a war on in Afghanistan, and if we don't contain it there, they'll bring it to the towns and streets of England, won't they? Al Quida is the threat. However long it takes, we've got to beat it. Stop worrying about the future, soldier, and learn to be proud. You're the backbone of your country."

My mind was very cool now, but I'd given over arguing. I thought calmly: so I'm a backbone, what about me arms and legs? Even if I knew how bricks were laid I couldn't lay them then, could I, how would I earn a living as a legless brickie? I tried to make a joke for him, to make him grin again, he'd started to look sort of sad. But I couldn't think of a way to put it.

There was silence for what seemed a good long while – just dim shouting from the square outside, a buzzing fly. Then the OC made a funny noise, a kind of brisk sound, as if the time had come to move it on. Ah well, I thought. Let's hear the worst. Glasshouse, would it be? Or Colchester, God forbleedingbid. Or just more punishment, more time as the sergeant's bitch?

But he hadn't finished yet completely, and he was still backtracking, in a way.

"Look, Tiny," he said, "we need soldiers don't we? That's the bottom line. That's why you joined up in the first place, I'm very sure of that, you were willing to risk your life – to *lose* it, even – for something that was right. And people around you now, people you don't rate, rough people, bitter people, vicious people, even – well, you'll be surprised, you'll be astonished at how they will turn out. They'll be soldiers. Some of them, believe me, will be heroes, fantastic, daring, terrific men. Good God, man, what's the alternative? Hitler had to be fought, didn't he? So did Saddam Hussein, Bin Laden, the insurgents. Someone had to be prepared to make the sacrifice. Am I right or am I wrong?"

I wished I'd had Shahid in with me. He could've argued back. The trouble was I did believe him. It was just...

"Yeah," I mumbled. "I suppose."

"And you suppose quite right, Hassan. The army's vital, and *you* are the army. You serve a useful purpose as a common soldier, and don't you let anybody tell you otherwise. You are a *hero*. Not potentially, but *now*. Because you're here. Because you're learning. Because you'll be prepared, when push comes to shove, to give your all. Your life. Do you agree?"

Oh, what a lovely question. Oh, what a prat. A hero or a dead hero. Was there any difference? What could I say? What was there left for me to say?

"Please, sir," I said. "What happens to me now? Is it the glasshouse? I'd really like to know, sir. Sorry."

He shuffled papers. He studied his screen. He put his finger ends together, and he smiled.

"Tiny," he said, "Potentially, I see you as a fine soldier – no, really, really fine. You're so unusual, such an *original* sort of chap, compared with the normal run of squaddie. Play it right, and all this will be forgotten, I can promise you." He tapped a single key with his finger, as if it was significant. He nodded, got dead serious. "It shouldn't affect your future career in any way. How does that sound?"

Like bullshit. Like total bullshit. I didn't say so, though.

"It'll have to go on your record, of course," he went on. "You understand that, don't you? But I can see no reason why that should cause you any grief, it's not even that unusual for certain lads to take time out these days. I'm very glad your father rang, though. I'm very glad he sent you back so promptly. And I'm inclined to believe you about that police girl, too. Like I said, I have you down as a good man, Tiny. Of great potential. Does that surprise you?"

It had surprised me that he even knew my name, quite honestly. But I knew the rules. I knew them better every day.

"Yessir. Thank you, sir."

"I have every confidence in you. I feel you'll work through this problem patch and go from strength to strength. I also understand your point about missing your comrades, especially Private Khan. After what you've said he sounds very interesting. Yes. very."

No mention of Ashton then, I noticed. But there's black and black, ain't there?

"Yessir. Thank you, sir."

He scratched his nose. Crunch time. Fine words, but now the punishment. I held me breath.

"I'm giving you a week's home leave," he said. He paused. "To get your head together. Does that sound fair?"

Fair? *Fair?* What could I say? 'Yessir, thank you, sir' didn't really cover it, did it?

But I was in the British Army. What could I do?

"Yessir, thank you, sir," I said.

And I mean that most sincerely, folks... I really do.

Here Comes the Bullet

One

The trouble with the army, is that nothing that you ever hear is true. Ever. In my time after basic training my mob were going – *for definite* – everywhere in the world that troops were stationed, and sometimes it changed three times a week. Afghanistan? Ireland? Iraq to sort out the shit we left there last time? – "yeah, deffo, it's official." Now the OC had told me we weren't going off to war – which meant we were – and here I was on a bloody train to Blackburn to see me mum.

And I wasn't on a charge, and the little crap-hat Jeff, Al Beano, Rick O'Shea, was not stone dead at all, but still alive and kicking in a civvie hospital.

Old Ken Rogers was dead for definite is what I'd heard first, and I'd got arseholed on the strength of it. Then Ken had told me it was Al, and this time it *was* for definite, he'd shot himself, "brains everywhere" – except he must'nt've had none, because he missed. Fair enough by me an' all – I didn't want to see him dead, why should I? – although I was a bit pissed off. If he hadn't topped himself, and made me think that he was Ken, I wouldn't have got wrecked and done a runner, and I'd've saved myself a lot of mither. On the other hand I'd got a week buckshee, and he'd got his life back, also. Which in the army – was probably not so bleeding good. The one thing that it proved for sure is that nothing's true, it's all a load of testicles, just don't believe a word the bastards say.

Anyway, the weather had dried up again, and the only black cloud on my horizon as the train clattered through the countryside was what line to shoot me mum and Vronnie. It'd only been about six weeks ago that I'd bullshitted I might be made up to lance quite soon, that everything was going great again, backtracking like a lunatic from being "negative." And now I had a black mark on my record, I'd be lowlife from here to Kingdom Come, and it was only by some sort of luck I hadn't been banged up for going AWOL. Oh Jesus – what if the Captain had rung up home to thank me "dad" in person for persuading me to go back? Oh Jesus, he still bloody might!

I stayed on until Manchester in the end, and I was wondering if to take the train back out again or go on the piss in town, when I saw some long fair hair I recognised – Emma. I called out, the way you do, and she turned round and smiled before I could regret it. She was in jeans and top and trainers and she looked so bleeding *normal*. I was in trackies and teeshirt, me, and scruffy as a tramp.

"Hi, Tiny. How you doing?"

"Hi. All right. You going home?"

"Yeah, been shopping. Coming on the train are you?"

So I made the big decision. Mum was half an hour away, and this girl who lived quite near our house was flirting, clear as daylight even to a prat like me, I couldn't go wrong.

"Nah, I think I'll stay in Manch," I said, going wrong as usual. I did a funny little smile. "I got some leave. Few days to see some mates."

She laughed.

"Suit yourself, general. Don't fancy you in civvies, any case. Ooh, I love that hat you wear!"

She was being nice still, and I should have laughed, and I felt gutted as I watched her nice arse walk away and climb up on the train. I felt gutted, and I felt a sort of empty anger, too. And then I felt an utter dickhead, so I went into a bar and got a drink and rung up Shofiq. By the time I got to his place I was pissed. Which got me out of seeing mum if nothing else, din't it?

I didn't see her next day neither, as it happened, nor the next one or the next. In fact the honest truth is, I didn't go home at all. Shof was living in a better part of Withington by now, a nice smart flat, and he had a nice smart girl-friend, too, a white girl called Sue. Me drunken bastard mate had gone legit, and when I sobered up they let me stay. Sue had a job, she had nice friends, and Shof was back at college, learning straight CT. Quite honestly, when I got a call from Sha and Ashton later in the week, it was a big relief. They'd finished in the south, they were coming back through Manch to have some drinking time, and were we going to meet? No way!

Naturally enough they were both pissed when they rung me, and you could hear them whooping down my mobile right across the flat. But there was no one there to bother except me, and I was out of there in minutes, and I didn't leave a note. Not far to Whalley Range by bus, and so what if it was pissing down again and I didn't have no coat? I was well 'ard, me – I was a soldier. And there'd be a floor to kip on, bound to be.

I had a funny sort of feeling, though, as I walked the last bit to the pub, it felt like there was something in the air. Shahid and Ashton drunk and noisy on the phone, little Carole in her bright white nightie with her legs tucked under her, so nice, so calm, so fucking kind, and Shofiq smart and sober in a proper flat, with Susie who tried to get me to ring my mum but only smiled when I said no. It felt like something weird was going on inside my head, and I didn't fucking like it. Manchester was full of civvies, and it wasn't Catterick.

I couldn't make more sense of it than that.

Two

There was something in the air for all of us that night, though, and as we went from pub to pub to pub, it seemed to bug us more and more. Ash, instead of getting randy, for once got sort of thoughtful, for example. It felt like something was coming out of joint.

"Legalise Crime," he said at one point, in response to absolutely bugger all. "That's my family motto, and it's the same for all us English blacks. It ain't our idea – we gets forced into it. For two good reasons."

"Oh aye," said Shahid. "Like that gang of hophead thugs back there?" We had moved out sharpish from the last place and were sitting in another heaving pub room with more pints of lager, getting hammered fast. "Name them, nigger boy."

Ashton pondered. He had a long weekend, he was on his home patch, and he'd get to shag his missus later on. He should have been delirious.

"Number One," he said, "all whities think we're criminals, which is rampant prejudice. And Number Two, they're right. No don't laugh, I fucking mean it. My Uncle Gilbert used to drive a bus when I were little, and he always called it his. How could he afford

196

that on his wages? A great big Magic Bus? He couldn't. He'd bloody knocked it off."

Was it the booze, or was he mental? We forgot to laugh. But Ashton, of the three of us, was the honestest in actual fact – or at least he hardly ever bent the law like we did – and it was giving him a bit of trouble, hence the jokes. He was under pressure, and he didn't know what to do about it. He might be getting in the shit.

The point was Sonia, the fiancée, had been down to visit him on the exercises, which should've been excellent. Except you don't do that sort of thing, do you, unless you've got a secret reason. Ulterior motive, that's what Shahid called it, and he was on the ball.

It was simple, really, when we got it out of him – she wanted him to quit. It was out of the blue to Ashton, a stroke of lightning, but logical to her, as clear as bleeding daylight. It was something to do with the way things were shaping in the 'Stan and crap, and (when he got it out of *her*) the marrying and babies and shite like that an' all.

"She said I'd have no chance with her if I got my cock shot off," he said, "which I reckon's fair enough, but she also said she'd been speaking to my cousins, which bloody ain't, it's strictly out of order. She said they'd give me a job at any time, good money, cash in hand, and as safe as bleeding houses."

"Nice work if you can get it, son," said Shahid, "but you're signed up for the full four years, ain't you? Who does she think you are? Houdini? How does she think you're getting out?"

"Catch Uncle Gilbert's Magic Bus," I said. No one laughed at that one, neither.

"Yeah, well I told her that, but she didn't believe me, women never do, do they? When I tried to get out dead legit in me first three months they knocked me back, and Sonia thought that that were my fault, too. For once it wan't, I were being straight, it were the army that was bent. I put me name down but they said I never did, or someone had lost the form or some such bollocks. And when I asked to go again they told me I was out of time, nobody's fault but mine. You can't argue with the office, can you? What's the point?"

"So what's your problem, then?" I asked. "She wants to you quit, but you can't for three more years. You'll still get your oats off her, don't say you won't, I don't believe you."

"But she thinks there's ways and means. And she thinks I won't try really, 'cause I don't want her to pin me down. She thinks I think she's out to trap me."

"Oh come on, Ash, you can't hardly wait, can you? And you can't get out, no way. You can't even do depression, you daft git!"

He smiled, and looked at his remaining mouthfuls. Ash couldn't do depression, except in twenty minute bursts. No contest.

"Yeah, but there's always other ways and means," he said, "I guess she's right at that. I mean, the thought of not having me legs blown off in Helmand's not a bad one, when you think about it, and it can mess the sex about when your girlfriend thinks you've got a death wish, silly cow. It's just the family bit that worries me. The family motto, like."

"Gawd, you and your family motto," Shahid said. He picked up the pots. "Same again, is it? I can take a bloody hint."

Squaddies always talk about how you can get out, it's one of them subjects that just comes up, like daytime telly and how bone the army is, and it don't mean a lot most of the time. But this time I could feel it really nudging, and I didn't really like it. Without Ash and Shahid in camp it had been terrible, and without Carole I'd probably be on the run by now, or more likely down Colchester in a cell.

More to the point, if Ash was thinking that way, you could be sure as shit that it was serious. Ash had a habit of getting things done, he didn't piss about. He slid his empty glass across to be refilled.

"D'you think you *could* get out then, Ash?" I said, as Shahid disappeared into the ruck. "What ways and means? I can't fucking think of none."

He looked at me and grinned. Relaxed as a newt, or would be pretty soon.

"You're too well brought up," he said. "My problem's this: what's worse, the army – crap food and getting shot at by the maniacs – or working with my bleeding cousins. You know what they're into, don't you? Cars. Ringing. High class motors, bent. Sonia can't see it, because they all wear classy suits, they don't do drugs, and me auntie's lovely! But I'm getting married soon, I've got me leave all booked. I don't want to spend me wedding night in Strangeways."

The trouble was with Ashton was, you never knew if he was joking, and when the lagers and the porky scratchings came, he didn't seem bothered about carrying the conversation on. I asked Sha if he'd been thinking of leaving as well as Ash since they'd been away down in the south, but he just shrugged.

"He talked about it, didn't he?" he said. "But why now? What's changed for me? I don't have no gorgeous white girl down on her knees begging me to quit. Down on her knees begging me for anything, more to the point. I'm a puritan, remember, I've been ruined by mad mullahs, I'm damn near a sex-free zone. Put it another way – situation normal. Same shit, different day."

"Well I dunno," I said. "I mean, I know where you're coming from, but I must say *I* feel different, kinda sort of, I feel like something might've changed." I paused. Picked up my new pint and chucked some down my neck. "Apart from anything else, I think I'm drinking myself to death. I'm serious. I'm losing days, Sha, I don't know if I'm on my tits or arsehole sometimes. I'm all fucked up."

"Like I said," he said. "Situation normal."

But he didn't laugh. He turned his head to Ashton.

"Are *you* still glad you signed up, nigger boy? Are you still…well, proud, like? To be in the army?"

Proud? What a word to use. But Ashton didn't fall about and spill his beer, surprisingly. In fact he held his pint up and looked at it as if it had some answers.

"In a way," he said. "I didn't realise what shit the money would turn out to be, like, and the government needs shooting for their fucking lies, but someone's got to do it, haven't they? And if it's either this or nicking Beamers, I dunno. I might stay in, whatever the 'ausfrau says. It keeps me off the streets."

Shahid was clocking me.

"You was quite chuffed with it when I first got to know you, Ti," he said. "You'd got fit, and off the dope, and you was the best shot in your company. If it's shit now it was just the same shit when you joined, weren't it? So what's changed? It or you?"

I had to think a while. I drank some lager and I crunched some porky scratchings. The others did, as well. A quiet little scene in a noisy, blaring pub.

"Maybe it's me," I said, at last. "Maybe that's its problem – it hasn't changed and it never fucking has to, does it? We'll be back up there on Sunday, won't we? And so will Mart, and Big Dave Hughes, and Chas Hicks and Timmo Hawes and Geordie George. Are you telling me that you can stand it? That everything's okay? SSDD and fucking hallelujah? That's bollocks, in't it? It's all so fucking bone."

Then Ashton dropped a casual little bombshell.

"Not Timmo Hawes," he said. He took a great big swig. "He's out. He's on his way. Got done for drugs, din't he? Class A."

That was a shaker, a real one.

"Timmo! Class A? But Timmo don't do drugs! Timmo *Hawes?*"

They both looked at me. Not amused, though, despite my ignorance.

"Yeah," said Shahid. "Funny, innit? Random drug test after the ranges one night, about a week ago. Timmo fails with knobs on. There were so much in his locker when they checked it after, they banged him in the glasshouse straight away. Timmo's out. I doubt they'll even let him back to Catterick."

I had to think that through. That sounded like a right old pile of crap. Timmo was a booze-hound, straight up and down. If he had a hero it was Homer, or maybe Homer and Barnie Gumble rolled into one. Can't get enough of that wonderful Duff!

"Maybe it was a plant?" I said. "Maybe someone down there had it in for him? Some southern bastard?"

Shahid nodded.

"Maybe it weren't. I mean, that camp were swimming in it, weren't it? If you wanted any, you'd never find a better bleeding place."

"But Timmo never did. Jeez, he was the biggest piss-head in the mob. Well, apart from all his mates. But drugs. Fuck me."

"Yeah," said Sha. "I tell you what though, Sherlock. We'll never know. Will we?"

"And it's bye-bye Timmo Hawes," said Ashton. "Sweet fucking dreams."

We'll never know. We'll never fucking know. But it makes you think though, doesn't it? It made us all think. Our brains were bloody boiling...

Three

Lance Corporal Martin was back on Sunday night, along with all the other buggers, and the new week started off the same as every other week – boring. Wake up, have shower, block jobs, breakfast, PT, TAB or circuit training, shower, change, do telly or the PlayStation, pie, chips, ignore the salad, sit around or get a game of football if your face fits, CFT Warrior, rifle cleaning, fall out. The only good bit was that I was off punishment ("Sarnt Williams said you was the best bitch he's ever fucked" – Martie) and the walking deadheads – which included Ken – had been cleared off to a different floor, or put down or something, they'd disappeared. The bad bit was that Gough was back next door, and I hated him. He'd got above himself, he'd got an attitude, and if he wasn't careful he'd get a fucking broken neck.

The only other good bit was we were going off to Wogland in a fortnight. Not a rumour, lads, it's definitely definite this time, that's definite. The 'Stan, or maybe somewhere else. And maybe it's two months, or on Wednesday afternoon. No time to even kiss the girls goodbye, best have one last little wank.

That first full evening back, the Monday, I went down to Ashton's room. I'd had me tea, which was shit, changed into civvies, boxed me kit away, polished me boots – ready for anything. Ashton had done the same, and bought some weed off someone in D Coy to start the evening off. He was in a really shitty mood, which was why he'd got the stuff, but he wouldn't really say what was bugging him. The posting news had sharpened up our minds a bit, but we hadn't done much more talking about leaving or stuff like that, there didn't seem a lot of point. We'd signed up for good or bad, and for the moment – well, that was that. So bugger it.

But his mood was quite annoying when I'd mellowed out a bit, so I said we'd better go out and get a drink down us. We signed off at the gate, and went to Tesco's for some brandy. Ash, as it happened, was due on ranges in the morning, but what the fuck? If he couldn't shoot an SA80 straight by now, no point in worrying.

We took nearly an hour to knock off the brandy – only half a bottle, all we could afford – and Ash was still dead moody until I finally dragged out of him that it was over money – his bank was playing silly buggers with his pay. He'd had a letter and a statement saying he was overdrawn, and charging him for the privilege, and he couldn't understand it. He showed me in the end, and it did look pretty bad – bleeding horrendous. But I couldn't see a mystery there, no way.

"Look," I said. "Check the dates. Two hundred out there. A hundred and forty there – that's two days later. Sixty seven out there. Sixty one. One fifty three. For fuck's sake, Ash, that's where it's gone, mate, and all them little 'OD's' mean overdrawn, don't they? So what d'you want to know?"

"Yeah yeah, I'm not bloody mental, prickface, I understand that, you twat. But all that *out*, and nothing fucking *in*, is there?" he said.

"No pay or nothing, not a fucking cent, what's that all about? Did you get paid this month?"

"'Course I did." I thought for a second. "Well, I spose I did, I never looked like, did I? I guess the bank'd tell me quick enough if I got skint."

"Too bloody right," he said. "That's what this letter says, innit? And they've charged another thirty quid for writing it, the bastards! But I haven't had me pay! It's gone missing!"

"It can't go bloody missing. Where's your slip?"

He looked at me. He made a funny face.

"I didn't get one. When I got this letter I went down the offices to kick up shit. They said it were a minor cock-up. Something in the system. It happens."

"Minor!" I shouted. "But you're getting charged interest by the bank, ain't you? Din't you tell them that?"

"Of course I fucking told 'em." Ashton sounded tired. "The corporal fucking laughed! 'Your problem, mate – change your fucking bank!' I went hairless. Shouting bloody murder. Sergeant come out in the end, give me a bollocking. He said he'd put me on Agai if I din't shut up."

We were in the pub by now, watering down the brandy in our bellies with some lager. Clerks hate squaddies. They love to screw things up for us, it's the way they get their rocks off, they're pathetic. They're fireproof an' all, though, untouchable. We drank and thought.

"What you going to do?" I asked. "Ring up your bank tomorrow? You might get more sense out of them. Well…"

He sighed.

"Nothing else I can do though, is there? 'Cept go back to the office grovelling. And hope the loot comes through and the bank don't sting me too much bloody extra charges." He sighed again, more like a groan this time. "It's this honeymoon," he said. "And then the wedding, when we gets round to it. It'll bankrupt me, but she ain't waiting too much longer. She wants to be a Mrs. Mrs Respectable."

I tried to cheer him up.

"Well, you black twats are always on about respect," I said. "You don't know what it fucking means, like, but you've got to have it, haven't you? If you're talking about suits and Rollers, mate, if you think that that's respect, it don't come cheap, though. Weddings are for mugs."

That didn't help much, I will admit. He was drinking very slow, as if that would make a difference to his debts. He kept looking at the statement, really bothered.

"We've booked two weeks in Cyprus," he said. "Arm and a leg job, Ti. All paid upfront, and now I've got to find some spends. Fucking nightmare. She's worth it, though, the slag. 'Ere, what about that Goughie, then?"

A change of subject. God knows where it came from, but thank God it did. He'd been looking suicidal.

"What about him? He still looks like the same old streak of piss to me."

"Yeah, 'course he is. He's been sucking up to the CSM they reckon, though. Bollocks Bowyer saw him with Colour and Mart Martin. Three peas in a pod, big mates. Because he took the rap for punching that police tart, maybe. Something cooking up."

I slid the last bit of my pint down. Looked at it significantly, like. He might be skint, but it was still his round.

"I thought *I* took the rap for that," I said. I knew what he meant though. If Gough was being sneaky it meant trouble, except I couldn't see what trouble there was left still to happen. We'd done our punishment, there wan't nothing left to cook. And every other bugger in the pikie fight had got away scot-free.

"Funny innit," I said. "He's gone from being everybody's kicking post to bleeding Supercreep. If he ever does go into action he'll get the VC, I'll put cash on it. Authentic British hero. No brains, no brawn, no fucking hope."

"Oooh, bitter!" said Ashton.

"No, lager," I said, quick as a flash. "And it's your shout, get 'em bloody in!"

That actually made him laugh, and he went off to the bar looking not so bloody glum. Through the door came Mart, and Big Dave Hughes and Bollocks, and Josh (whose sister does), and Billy 'Unt – and Goughie. Thick as thieves they were, and twice as friendly. Except that Gough got in the drinks, and all of them had pints with double whisky chasers. Not much friendship there then, whatever the poor sap thought. They took up the tables next to ours.

"Yo, bitch!" Mart said to me. "How's the battered bumhole?"

There was a bit more banter when Ash came back, but Martie was too dumb to dredge up much, and it fizzled out. They were already a bit rowdy, and they settled down to get the pissedness level up, with the corporal shouting off about some "master plan" he had. Pity we'd just got drinks in, we could've buggered off. No problem, though. A pint don't last that long.

We'd lost our will for conversation – our will to live, you could say – but we heard pretty damn soon what Martin had in mind. It seemed he'd got his taste for trouble fired up down south, he'd been in punch-ups every other night, and his face was all cuts and bruises, some half-healed. Maybe the CSM was in on it. Maybe that's what the crack had been. And there was more crack looming.

"I know you don't give a fuck for footie, la'," he said to Bollocks." But it's the big one, see. There's Jocks involved. There could be well good trouble."

Oh, football. Boring. That's what Bowyer thought, and he'd need some convincing this time, you could tell.

"Yeah," said Bollocks, "fair enough, but the Jocks *ain't* involved though, are they? It's England against some fucking team, they're all the fucking same to me – but it ain't the fucking Scotch. So where's the fucking trouble coming from?"

"It's Gough's idea," said Mart. "Nice one, Goughie, fucking smart, la'. We goes into Darlington and hits the sports shops, and we gets all their foreign flags, every last one in the bleeding town. What is it, Portugal we're playing? Some gang of fucking wops, who cares? We're all supporting England, okay, everyone's supporting England except the Jocks, who'd rather bleeding die, so we flogs them all the wog gear to dress up in on the night! They're thick, okay, but they'll get the idea in the end, won't they – they can be the official fucking opposition! It's trouble guaranteed!"

I saw Goughie's adam's apple bob up and down. He was going to speak! Daring...

"Especially if we give 'em at half price," he said. "I mean, you know what Jocks are over money."

"Fuck off!" said Big Dave Hughes. "Them fucking foreign strips cost dosh, mate. Half price? You must be fucking joking!"

Billy 'Unt said: "Don't be stupid, Dave, we don't pay for 'em do we, where's your regimental pride? The Jocks pay *us* half price, we pay the shops sweet bugger all. We go in mob-handed, create diversions, out like a dose of salts with all the gear. Or you can tell the shopgirls you're Wayne Rooney, looking for a freebie. You look like fucking Shrek!"

"Who's Shrek?" said Big Dave Hughes, and he wasn't joking, either. "What for, anyway? Why the foreign flags, and that? Ain't we supporting Ingerland?"

"Course we are, you dildo! And the Jocks support the enemy! England's enemy, don't matter who it is, it's in the blood, innit? We get their money for the strips that cost us nothing, and we get an 'omemade war. Jesus, Dave. You are so, so thick. Get 'em bloody in."

The match was in the Naafi, on the big screens, and someone sprung the idea on the Scotchmen a day or two before, fed it to 'em like some deadly secret. I don't know who did the spreading of the virus – Colour I think – but he played a blinder. Suddenly there was Jock lads everywhere – sworn to secrecy among themselves, the halfwits – getting opposition shirts, and flags, and coughing up real loot if they couldn't nick or beast them out of someone – to wear under normal, neutral stuff and infiltrate into the game on Saturday. They thought it was all their own idea, that was the best thing. They were going to time it to the second, wait for a signal, then switch from being Scottie squaddies into foreign football fans rooting for the dagoes – and screw the English to the fucking floor. It was a dead sweet plan, I must admit.

Then, two days before the match, fucking disaster. Out of the blue, out of a fucking cloudless sky, Shahid and Ashton both got knocked back. An army carve-up, pure and simple, and both of them completely blown away. Ashton's leave was cancelled – his pre-wedding honeymoon, his fortnight in the Cyprus sun – and Shahid was pulled in by the RMPs. They wouldn't tell him why – why should they? – but everybody knew, him most of all. Ashton was flattened, he was in the lower fucking depths. Shahid was so angry I swear he turned damn nearly white. And Goughie was behind it, it was obvious. Who fucking else?

The upshot was, that quitting came back in the air for us, big time. Four years to serve? Not fucking much! Ashton was so livid it's a wonder he didn't go straight over the wire the day he got the news, and as for Shahid, he just vanished off the block. Now you see him, now you don't. The disappearing Paki.

So just like that I'm on me Jack again, the second time in no damn time at all. It made me think what it'd be like out there, Afghanistan, Iraq, even Iran if our Yankee masters decide we'll give them some "democracy" as well. If I got a bullet in the head, fair enough – I'd be a hero, mum could be proud of me at last, and at least the army don't charge you for your funeral yet, though it's bound to happen some day I suppose.

But if Ash and Sha got killed – or if they did a runner, or got sent to jail for treachery – I'd be on my own again, full time.

Fuck that for a game of soldiers.

Four

L ike I've said before, you're taught to hate everyone except the
men in your own mob from the first day of training almost. But
when it comes to it, even people with a natural hatred for each other,
like Manks and Scousers, Lanks and Yorkies, can join together to
fuck off a common enemy. The civvies, say, the Taffs and Brummies
and the southerners. And the Jocks.

Before we even passed off of the square, before we swapped crap
hats for badge and beret, we knew half a dozen chants about the
kiltie-men which were bound to lead to fights, and we used them
every where, and every way, we could. That meant fights on the
block, fights in the lines, fights on the ranges, in trains and buses,
fights in Catterick, even the sergeants in their mess. When I say
we, I don't mean me, particular, I wasn't that bothered much. I just
mean us. The good guys versus them.

So when we crowded in the Naafi for the match, the air was like
electric, it was jumping. The Scotchmen kept the flags and strips
we'd sold 'em hid from us (thinking they were so fucking crafty!), and
our fanatics looked like butter wouldn't melt, they looked like lickle
fucking angels. Ooh, there was going to be a holocaust!

It didn't come off quick, that would have spoiled it. In any case, the
actual game, far as I could tell who don't give jack shit for football,

213

was too boring to get up much extra buzz, enough to tip from
tension to a fucking bang – at least until the booze kicked in. But
with both my mates out of circulation, let's just say that I was bored.
Too bored to stay away from bloodshed, too bored to wander round
the empty town, but also too bored to notice who the actual side
was that licked old Ingerland. Portugal? Yeah, that was it maybe.
Although I could be wrong. But they did lick us, although it took
them long enough. And when they did – and by then the booze was
running down the throats like water – the Jocks went wild. They
erupted like volcanoes. Volcanoes on the piss...

They did it sudden, like, and the way they whipped their hidden
flags out, and stripped their tops off down to the foreign, winning
shirts, was a touch of pure, wicked, evil, magic. One instant they
were England fans, down in the mouth and disappointed like the
rest, and the next they were foreign nutters, waving their colours,
whooping and shrieking like bloody dervishes.

"Ye wank-airs! Ye wank-airs! Fuck the English! Fuck the English
fairies! Scawe'land f'r'evair!"

Well everybody knows the Jocks are hardest, that's ancient history.
They're not the biggest, they're not the brightest, they sure as shit
are not the best. But fired up by coke and whisky, the little bonehead bastards are unbeatable. They swept across the Naafi floor like
a horde of devils pouring out of hell, and a hail of glasses sailed in
front of them. They bounced off everything, the ones that didn't
smash, off the chairs, the ceiling, mirrors, regimental photographs,
off the fruit machines, and people's heads, and soon the walls were
pissing blood and lager. Some optic bottles got smashed behind

the bar until the shutters were crashed down, and one of the telly screens went off with a bang and flash.

The Jocks are hardest, man for man, but this fight was about numbers, as much as anything. All the English buried the hatchet, so to speak, then looked for a Scotch head to bury it in again, and for the first phase everybody went by colour. England flags, tied around necks like capes, went rushing at the foreign flags, then at Scottish crosses that got conjured out of nowhere. I saw one Jock almost strangled by a Union Jack that two squaddies twisted round his neck and pulled till he went purple.

Then it got sectarian, in a way – one group of Proddie Glasgows who'd been supporting England (for real) got turned on by the Celtic fans. They teamed up with the little Welsh contingent ("Free Wales with every twenty litres," as the petrol slogan used to say), but some Irish Guardsmen decided they hated the Taffs more than they liked the Catholics and soon it was a free for all.

Not everyone was fighting. Not me, for starters – I like my anger personal – and it was easy to avoid if you kept your brain switched on. I quit after about ten minutes, but before I got back to the lines I was overtaken by lads from the Naafi who were foaming at the bleeding mouth, and then I passed them rushing back into the fight again two minutes later with knives they'd picked up in their rooms, and madness in their pissed-up little eyes. Not long after that the barking started, and the RMPs turned up in droves and went in with the dogs. Then blokes came running back towards the blocks with blood and slobber on them, and their trackies torn to buggery.

After that, more or less, it became a spectator sport. Lots of us just stood about and watched the dogs and MPs chase the squaddies, then sometimes the squaddies chase each other or the dogs. Big Dave told me that the corporals in the mess were having the same fight on their home ground, and he said he'd seen Mart Martin smack another lancejack with a waffle. Yeah, a waffle, not a bottle, that's what Big Dave said, and I didn't like to comment. But I did hear Sarnt Williams forcing some lads back when he saw them sneaking off. "Oi," he said. "Don't you know there's a war on? Go and get the Jock cunts, you lazy little bastards!"

It was reckoned later that the fight went on for two full hours, but that don't seem very likely in my book. But there was skirmishes and boozing late into the night though, I'll grant you that, and Catterick that evening was not the sort of place you'd want to take your granny for a cocktail, even though a good half of camp couldn't get passes out for love or money. The shouting and the smashing up of furniture in the rooms and corridors got right on Ashton's tits because of his mood, and when I saw him he was furious and kept muttering that we ought to tell the papers, to let the outside world see just what shit the army really is. He'd been on the phone for two days on and off, to the fiancée mainly, and the bank, and quite honestly he didn't know what to do.

"Our boys!" he said. "That's what they're always on about, the Daily Mail and shit, our marvellous, wonderful, fantastic fucking boys. And they treat us like animals, and that's what we fucking are! Our fucking, fucking *boys*! It needs shutting down, Ti. It all needs fucking shutting down."

And not much later, when he'd cooled off a bit, and I'd persuaded him to have a suck or two out of a tin, he said, "I'm running, mate. I've had enough. I'm gone."

"Shit, Ash," I said. "But why, though? I mean, like, where to?"

"Why? Because I've changed me mind, you dick. Why? D'you really have to fucking ask? I can't do it, Ti. I can't stay here no more, I'm off for bleeding good. I'll go up and hide with Carole and the girls in Newcastle, the RMPs won't look for me up there. The girls'll put me up okay till Manchester's clear of the bastards, won't they? They'll see me right."

"She'll bleeding kill you, mate."

"Who? Carole? Why?"

"Not Carole, you twat, bleeding Sonia. You've lost your honeymoon already. What good will it do to go on the run? She'll see you even less, won't she?"

They'd sprung the honeymoon disaster in the way they do these things to squaddies – just in a sudden meeting that they'd called us to, the whole damn lot of us, not just poor old Ashton. We'd been sat down and left waiting in a room for half an hour, then an officer and a sergeant had waltzed in, all smiles, and announced that "normal scheduling was up in the air" – i.e. cancelled – because we "might be moving out."

Moving out, sir? Where, sir? Why, sir? When? No answer, there's never any answer – but mysterious smiles, as usual. We'd find out "soon enough."

Ashton had went hairless.

"Soon enough, sir! But I've got leave, sir! It's booked, sir! I'm going on my honeymoon to Cyprus! I've had the dates for weeks!"

The bringer of bad tidings was only a second lieutenant, about ten years old, but smugger than a newly-polished arsehole. He'd looked at Ash like he was the lowest form of life.

"Getting married are we, Private? Is this official? Do the office know?"

Like buggery they did. Marriage wasn't in it, for the moment, it was not official in Ashton's book. Just the honeymoon. His fury grew. You could see it building up inside him. His tongue was tying up in knots.

"But I'm off, sir! It's been cleared for weeks! I'm going Cyprus with me girlfriend!"

"Your girlfriend or your wife? Is there some confusion in your mind?"

Everyone was laughing, naturally – kick a bugger when he's down. Ashton tried to speak again, but lost his words.

"But sir," he said. "But sir, I mean – but sir, the whole fu…but it were all fixed up, sir. The whole… I've *paid*!"

Oh how happy did that make the young lieutenant! How *happy*.

"We'll I'm sorry, Private, you know the rules. You're in the army 24/7, you can't just take time off because you fancy it. Good heavens – we're at war. They need us out there. They need fresh blood, fresh bone, fresh sinew. We can't stop so that you can get some shagging in, can we, be reasonable! This could be your chance to be a hero, and think how proud your girlfriend'd be then! Much more exciting than a honeymoon, I can tell you."

End on a joke, that's the golden rule. The unfunnier the better (though that one was worth the laugh it got, fair play). But it was the end, Ashton didn't get the chance to witter on for longer, the sergeant made it clear he'd play the heavy if need be, the time had come. We trooped out in silence, and Ashton was the silentest of all.

Over the next two days, though, he forced himself not to just give it up completely. He spoke to everyone he could, hung round the offices, wheedled the liaison clerk, the RSM (tried to see him; failed), he even thought of writing to his MP, except he didn't know he had one, or if he did do, who it was or how he could find out. The upshot was, the simple fact, the inevitable, unvarnished truth – he was fucked. It had started with a minor row with some pay clerk corporal about his overdraft, we were all agreed on that. But you can't ever prove it, can you? It's just one of those little army things.

After the riot, as we sat drinking Stella in his room and listening to the chaos still going on outside, he brought me up to speed. "I've been onto the travel agents three times again today," he told me. "I tried to get my money back, or switch the dates, they told me to piss off. That's why I'm going, Tiny. Too many bastards saying just piss off. Well I am. I'm leggin' it."

"Life of crime, mate," I said. "Ain't that what you said you was afraid of?"

I thought that he might dob me one, but then he laughed.

"D'you know, mate," he said, "I joined up first to keep me *from* a life of bleeding crime. I had to earn a living and I couldn't do nowt else, there weren't nothing. Now I'm destitute, even if I fucking stay. I can't *afford* to fucking stay. Fourteen grand a year, mate, and I'm meant to get married on it. I'm gone. I'm getting out of here."

Like I've said before, when Ash reckons to do something, it gets done. I had a growing feeling in my stomach. I was getting right pissed off.

But I didn't have another word to say.

Five

Shahid's case, when we finally got to see him again on Sunday night, turned out to be completely different. We hadn't seen it happen, but he'd been lifted by the RMPs on Friday and given five to pack a bag, they'd been as crafty as a gang of shithouse rats. The story later, that went round the lines, was he'd been fingered by Goughie as a Muslim terrorist, and was took off to be shot. We didn't buy that shite, we knew Shahid too well, but we wondered how he'd wriggle out, big style. And in fact, he said – he'd gone to get promoted.

He came back into my room about eight o'clock, where me and Ash were drinking, and he looked pretty pale, for an Asian. Ashton was still depressed – he'd picked a fight with a lancejack office clerk after the Sunday service and was probably on a charge next morning – and I was getting that way too. The whole deal seemed just pointless, ridiculous, it was like a bear pit, not a bleeding army. And I'd heard as well that old Ken Rogers had just got "sent away."

"Christ, where you been, Sha?" I said. "We thought you'd been locked up in the fucking Tower and that was that. Didn't they believe you were in love with Alkie Ada after all?"

He threw his bag down on a bed, and picked up a can of lager.

"I ain't been no farther than the other side of town," he said. "I tell you, when they do exotic, they do it bloody marvellous. They didn't even have halal meat for me."

"You don't eat halal," said Ashton. "What you on about?"

"It's the principle, you twat! They were trying to butter me up, weren't they? They wanted to get me on their side. And they couldn't even work out that Muslims don't eat roast pork."

"But you do eat pork," Ashton gives it. "I've fucking seen you!"

"Oh shut up, Ash," I said. "If you don't get it, just shut up, why don't you? There's more Stella in me locker, get some out. Shahid – who did it to you? Was it Goughie? Who was there? Was it the ginger bastard?"

He looked at me as if I'd gone stupid, too.

"Were it fuck as like. I told you, din't I? It was the Captain, and two blokes from somewhere else. In civvies, but I figured out they must be special branch or summat, although I don't think they'd ever met a proper Paki face to face. They asked me if I spoke Arabic. I said a bit of Urdu, I din't bother with the loonies at the mosque no more. That seemed to perk 'em up a bit. They asked me what I thought about religion."

"Bloody hell," said Ash. "Lecture time. I bet you bored the bastards half to death."

"Hope so. I don't think so, though. They seemed to be a bit pissed off more like it. I said I thought anyone who believed in God was pretty much insane in my opinion, whatever name they called the bastard by. The OC went bright red. But one of the civvy men goes 'At least Christians don't blow their fellow men to pieces, do they,' and I gives it, 'I thought that's what the army paid us for.'"

"Fuck me," said Ashton. "You din't really did you, Sha? You bullshitter."

"Well, it were something like that," said Shahid. "We talked round and round in bloody circles, it went on for ages. Most of the time I din't know what they were trying to say, it was like in riddles. They asked me what I thought of terrorists, I know that much. And if I thought suicide bombers had a point. We know all about suicide bombers, us Pakis. You ask anyone."

"Jesus," I said. "What did you say?"

"I said I were a bloody Asian, not insane. I said that's why I joined the army, weren't it – because I were worried sick about poor dicks who listened to the Stone Age mullahs and blew up people in the street and fucking babies in the name of fucking Allah. Din't say fucking, come to think of it, but I nearly did. I were getting kind of mad with 'em although I still didn't realise what they were driving at, exactly. Then the OC put me right, poor bastard. I hadn't really noticed till then what a prat he is, ain't he? He is really, really thick."

"They all are," Ashton said. "That's how they get the job. They're mental."

"Yeah well," Sha goes. "He used that word an' all. He told me Muslims are mental, borderline insane, he actually said that, then he said, 'not all of them, of course, not all of you!' And then he goes, 'you must agree?' The funny thing is, he was trying to make it better. He was trying to make me understand the problem. Then he must've saw my face, and he goes: 'I'm not a racist, Khan, of course, but...'"

Even Ashton fell about at that.

"Not a racist but what, for Christ's sake?" he hooted.

"He lost his thread a bit," Sha said. "He were embarrassed, like. *He* wan't a racist, he goes on, but lots of 'my lot' *were,* maybe. Well, pretty sort of crazy, anyway. Funny ideas. Worshipped a sort of... The upshot was, the army needed guys like me. Role models. Example to the fruitloops to get real. Did I agree? The others didn't help him out much, they looked at him as if he was a proper twat, I were almost tempted to tell them I agreed with him. Then one of them come out with it. The giveaway that they were special branch or something."

He necked the tin and took a good long pull.

"'If it's really why you joined the army, Mr Khan,' he gives it, 'if it's because of worrying about extremists an' all that, how would you like to do a little bit more? For your country. I take it you see yourself as British, do you?'"

"Cheeky bastard," Ashton says. "I bet he wan't born in fucking Oldham like you wa'!"

"*Mister* Khan though, eh," I said. "It's a start Sha, innit?"

Sha carried on, despite the piss-takes.

"'A little bit more what?' I asks him. 'A bit more persuading Muslims to join the army? Or just spying on my mates? I see myself as English because I bloody am, and I joined to show some people we're not all fucking mad. Is that what you're saying? Sleeping with the fucking enemy?'"

"Good film that," said Ash. "Is that the one where you get to see her cunt?"

"If you want to see a cunt," I said, "look in the mirror, Ashton, the professor's talking. Go on Sha. What'd he say then? I'm listening."

Sha shook his head. And Ashton only grinned.

"Oh, he asked me if I knew there was a war on. A fucking war on terror, you know, east v. west. Democracy. Teaching human rights to backward nations, great things like that. I said I didn't know what great things he meant. Half a million civilians killed in Iraq, maybe? Bombing raids from unmanned drones, wedding parties our speciality? What's that teaching anyone? Except they've got to fight us to the fucking death. I asked him if he'd ever thought of that."

He took another slug of lager.

"And then I said we're going to lose," Sha said. "Even the Yanks have give a sort of date, which means they're moving out whatever state they leave the country in, and we stay till then or even later, their loyal fucking poodle. We're only hanging on to save a bit of face, we had no pissing right to be there in the first place, and the more Muslims get killed, the more Muslims'll try and kill us in revenge. And fighting an invader ain't illegal, in anybody's book."

"Pissing hell," said Ashton, when Shahid ran out of steam. "Did they call a redcap in? You'll get done for treason you will, Sha."

"I wouldn't be surprised. They started muttering and mumbling, and one asked me how I could claim to be a loyal soldier if I thought we'd got the whole thing wrong, and how dare I say it wa' illegal which it bloody wan't, and how the fuck would I know? I stared him out. I said I'd changed my mind, and a loyal soldier who saw something wrong were duty bound to say so, surely, it were logical. I said I joined up because I thought we *weren't* the enemy, we wa' there to do a proper job, and if I'd realised… Oh I don't know, I sort of packed up then, I were getting me knickers in a twist. I thought one of them wa' going to hit me, in actual fact. He went black, it were amazing."

"Black?" said Ashton. "I knew they couldn't be completely bad!"

"Fuck off, daft twat," said Shahid, but he had to laugh. "Anyway, you ain't heard the best bit yet. The OC agreed with me, the gutless pillock! He said a soldier had to think, it was how you could pick a good 'un from the rest. And he said he'd brought me in to make me up to lancejack!"

This was a real stunner. Me and Ashton goggled.

"He didn't?" Ashton breathed. "What, you a lance? Lance Corporal Fucking Khan?"

Shahid emptied the Stella can. And crushed it with both hands.

"Not likely, is it? I'd like to say I turned it down, but I never got the offer. He just said he'd *brought me in to –* and told me what I'd missed because of my attitude! The other two nodded like two clockwork arseholes, but they didn't dare to smile. Then the OC said 'Better luck next time,' and they both muttered something and he went bright red again. From where I were sitting, I'd say my future in the army don't look very bright. What d'you reckon, lads?"

He clicked a ring-pull open and took a hefty slug. He didn't seem right bothered.

Ashton said another funny thing. It must've been his day for it.

"You're better out of it, ask me," he said. "Whatever they say they hate your lot worst of all, deep down. But just because you keep your arseholes pointing west to pray, don't mean you're arseholes, does it? 'Ave you ever thought of driving cabs?"

Shahid smiled.

"What about your uncle what nicks buses? Could he get me one, if you have a word with him?"

"They wouldn't let you go, though, Sha," I said. "It would look terrible for the army racial quota figures, wouldn't it? Bloody Ada, Ash'd be the only black twat left, except for Wasambu-Sambo – and he's a bleeding foreigner!"

"Aye, well I ain't hanging round if Shahid goes," laughed Ashton. "If they can see you as a lancejack, Sha, they'd make me up to general if I was the last one left, wouldn't they! Oh Christ, the responsibility! No way. No fucking way…"

Which only left one question, as far as we could see. We'd need more Stella. We'd need to put our bloody minds to it.

Three Ways to Leave the Army

One

That was it, really, for all of us – although I'm not saying there was anything dicey about the way we did it, you never know who's listening do you, and you never know how long the army's memory is. The fact is that we did. We got the bullet. Three bullets, three of us. It was pretty neat.

Put it another way we all got out of there, and it was honest and legitimate, and all above the board, and if anybody questions us, we know the answers to every question, don't we? All for one and one for all was what the three musketeers reckoned, according to Dogtanyan, and we stuck together, we were a team through thick and thin. It ain't so easy to get out these days, although joining up's a piece of piss since only fucking royalty and other low grade morons want the job. They've raised the age bar to include geriatrics, white sticks are standard issue if you drive a tank, and they take green men from outer space. Funny to think that fifty years ago there was a colour bar. Ashton and Sha would've been laughed out of the recruiting office.

What did for me – and I swear to you this was not a put-up job – was another piece of army lunacy. There was a random drug test due on the Thursday, I took it like I always did because I knew that I was clean – and failed. I don't do drugs, see? I used to work in a needle exchange, I spent time with crackheads and no-hopers, I even slept with a poor neurotic bitch from Portavogie. To pass the time I'd done some bits of dope maybe, a tab of E or two sometimes, but all the random tests I'd ever gone to I'd passed A1. And this one wan't no different.

Most people in the camp who don't do drugs take the random tests, and they always pass, surprise surprise. Sometimes people who do do drugs get randomed by mistake, and fail. I figure that's quite reasonable. If they're so off their face they don't notice when one's due, it makes sense that they should leave the army. After all, some of the weapons they give us to play about with can be very dangerous, can't they? Ask Al Beano, Jeff, the one that tried to find his brain and missed.

The point is about the tests, is that they're random, which in army logic means that every bugger knows just when they'll be. So if you don't do drugs you go along to get some free time off, and if you do you don't. You go hiding in the bog, you get busy, you do a CFT. There were lads on my lines who could hardly walk and talk some days, and as far as I know they're still lobbing RPGs at ragheads in the sand. If they'd ever had a test the lab technicians would have fainted, or sold syringes of their samples down the clubs for rocket fuel. But they didn't have a test, because they damn well knew the rules. I went along this Thursday as per usual, innocent as a new-born babe. And failed.

Would you believe it?

It was a real big shock this was, as I told my mother on the phone, a mistake, a mystery, some sort of army snafu that I couldn't understand. Why would I do it, mum, I said – when the OC called me to his office I honestly thought I was going to get promotion like they'd offered Shahid Khan, my mate. I was one of the good guys. I always had been.

The funny thing was, was the drug I got picked up for. The OC said it was cocaine, and the test was definite. I asked if I could have a second test, on the same sample, and he said I could if I paid three hundred pounds, and the result would be the same, they always were. He asked me, if I said I hadn't done it, how it could have been there, so positive? I said I didn't know. And when I thought about it, I cited the football riot and the piss-ups that had followed on. My sister Vronnie said it was the "drug of choice" these days for spiking people's drinks. Her best friend's mum, a nurse at the infirmary, said they did dozens of young kids every weekend. It was an epidemic.

Vronnie rung me up later, in actual fact, and said "Nice one Tiny, but wouldn't pot have been a cheaper way to go?" A fucking cynic in the family. You've got to laugh though, an't you?

She'd've been dead wrong in any case, because the times they were a changin', which was another funny thing. When I'd joined the army, not so bleeding long ago, you could get chucked out for soft stuff like weed or dope, or even getting ratted once too often. Now though, it was only the hard gear that they bothered with, and after a few more years in the Sandpit, if we last that long out there, you'll have to be so full of drugs you'll go off like a bomb when they stick a needle in to test you. Otherwise, according to Shahid, they'll be so short of cannon fodder they might even have to stop the fucking war – or call up Tony Blair's kids, ha ha ha.

Drugs or no drugs, though, they took a damn long time to let me go, compared with Sha, who got out like lightning with a very sudden case of acute religious persecution. Dead true in one way, I suppose, because it must have really pissed them off the way he pissed on them. He'd gone to see the Padre bold as brass, and said he was going to become a member of the Wahhabi sect, was that all right? The Major had to say he was delighted, naturally – all faiths welcome here, my son, even if I've never heard of 'em – till Sha kindly spelt it out. Wahhabis are the gang of nutcases who think that all non-members, including other Muslims, have to be killed off as a sacred duty because old Allah said so (but only to a Wahhabi, naturally). So next time he got issued with an SA80 and a clip, said Sha, he'd have to shoot down all his mates, unless they converted on the spot. Plus officers. Plus Padres.

"But why?" goes Canon Fodder.

"Because blood is thicker than water!" Sha gives it. "It is written! And the Koran Q'ran't be wrong!"

We all knew he didn't mean it, and maybe they did too, but how could they prove a thing like that? They questioned and questioned him, and he never cracked a smile. He went everywhere carrying his good book and never changed his story by a single word. He left ten weeks before I did, although they kept him waiting months and months and months for the pay that they still owed him, the office clerks' revenge, sad twats. He's not a terrorist, though, however hard they tried to make him. In fact I think he still tries to talk sense into pissed-off young Muslims outside mosques from time to time, and sometimes they beat him up for it. When I asked him why he bothered he said he had a sense of duty.

"That's why I joined the army in the first place, innit? I thought if we could stop foreign Muslims wasting other foreign Muslims' blood it might stop brainwashed English Muslims flocking out from here to kill Yank and British squaddies – and other Muslims. Stop English Muslim dickheads putting bombs on trains and planes and buses full of other English Muslims. I were born in Oldham, Tiny, it's full of English Muslims and it's my fucking home. England's where I fucking live."

"But the army chucked you out!" I said. "You joined, and then you couldn't stand the bastards any more, they drove you into quitting! And I mean, it was us lot that invaded in the first place, wan't it? You can see their point in some ways. Even I can, for Chrissake!"

"Their point, my point, your point, whose point, Tiny? That's what's fucking bugging me. They killed three thousand on 9/ll, and we killed five hundred thousand just to pay 'em back in a country that weren't involved to start with. Mad enough for you? Try this: My sister still thinks the Muslims had nowt to do with the Twin Towers, it were a Jewish conspiracy. And when you ask her a conspiracy to do what, how dare I question Allah's will? And she wants to be a teacher, Tiny, she wants to mess with children's minds. Maybe we started it, but it's Muslim killing Muslim now, and maybe it always will be. What is it? Are we stupider than you lot? We can't be, can we? What's the fucking reason?"

We had a fair few conversations like this these days, and Shofiq and Susie down in Withington, where I'd gone to live now, sometimes joined in, too, they'd got to be good mates. It made me feel a bit ignorant to tell the truth, and Shof and Ashton couldn't take too much of it, but Sue and Shahid argued black was blue, because she said she'd been a Catholic and knew where he was coming from, and said that both of them was "damaged goods." She said the Muslims' problem in Britain was simple – they still thought God was real, and couldn't believe the British didn't and might be bloody right.

"It's not stupidity," she told him, "You've been conned, indoctrinated. And one day you'll all wake up and realise they've been telling you porkies, just to keep you where they wanted you, and then you'll slowly come all right. Your mullahs, the men who know it all, the men who get it straight from God – they'll end up like our priests in Ireland, brain dead with whiskey and a nice fat housekeeper who gives a lovely handjob when the need arises, so to speak. When my dad was young, every other son in every other house in Ireland was sent to train to be a priest, and now they have to bring them in from Poland, like the plumbers and the plasterers. It's brainwashing, Sha, all brainwashing. Get over it and find yourself a sex-mad English girl. She'll teach you what religion's all about! Shofiq knows!"

Ashton's way out had been the most spectacular, although it could have blown up in his face big style, but he was getting desperate. He didn't trust the drugs thing, religion was a no-go, and he thought his scheme was foolproof anyway. First off he nicked a car one night, completely pissed, no licence, no insurance, no cock-all, and demolished a bus shelter just by the camp, his get-out from the army, guaranteed. But although he got a mega bollocking, the army kept the cops away and covered up for him, like they could do brilliant if they wanted to. He was a quota-boy, remember, one of the ethnics, one of the few, as Winston Churchill put it. And he could hardly tell them it was done deliberate, could he?

Insubordination, insolence, farting in church – after that he tried the lot, and got damn all down them roads, neither. Three days in cells, one severe beating off Sergeant Williams and Martie Martin, two painful sessions at the dentist for his broken teeth.

When he was totally pissed off with all the duff attempts, he "changed the habits of a lifetime," and got his cousins to set up a failed "robbery" – and bloody nearly got sent down, because they cocked it up. Luckily his fiancée stood by him – she was pregnant with their little girl – and she looked so respectable in the witness box, so nice and demure, so very, very white, that they damn nearly let him stay in the regiment as well, which would have been the worst disaster in his life! He'd asked me to be another character witness, as it happened, and I told him not to be so bloody mad – unless he wanted to go down, to avoid the wedding that he'd still not managed yet. After pleading guilty – probation, and a promise to go straight – he did go straight, as well. Still beats me at pool.

It took me ages to actually get out, to get clear of the garrison, they kept me hanging round for yonks while they fooled and faffed about, and it must have cost the country hundreds in wages and that sort of stuff. It was all free time for me as well – they couldn't let me do anything, least of all get me fingers on a weapon "while under discharge orders" – but the wankers in the office couldn't get it together, no way, except to wind me up. I got lots of weekends off, though, and me and Emma took up finally, although she finishes with me if I ever lose my temper, which is terrific training after all the shite they've piled on me. As well as basic IT stuff with her, I'm going back to college soon, to train up for some sort of job. Shofiq and Susie have been brilliant.

The others in my army life, I must say, have faded from my memory pretty fast, and pretty far, and I don't regret their going for a bleeding moment – because I didn't make so many proper mates, did I? On the other hand, I don't regret signing in the first place neither, come to think of it. I needed something to give me life a kick up the arse, and it did some great things for me, too, until I messed it up. I got a lot of strength, a lot of fitness, even a bit of confidence, in a funny sort of way. And that's growing all the time.

I feel pity for the poor sods that are still there though, especially the halfwits that don't even know they're being screwed and slaughtered to save some bastard's face. And I can't help feeling sorry for the ones I see on telly, brown, and hard, and active, and looking like their weapons are a part of them, like they're some sort of a brilliant, natural, human man-machine, born and bred to fight.

For some lads it's dead good, I'll go along with that. Some lads love it, some lads think it's mint. And in a way, I sometimes wish I could have ended up like that, I feel maybe I could have done if things had turned out different. I feel sorry for them, with just a little touch of jealousy. And then I look at mum, and Vron, and Emma, and I think.

I think: Let's just hope they're not the ones who have their cocks shot off and find their only helpers are the social and the NHS. Let's just hope they're not the ones who get sent away from hospital with a bunch of pamphlets for depression and go back home and butcher up their mum and dad. Let's just hope they're not the ones whose families have to sue the government to get half the compensation they shell out for a typist with a broken fingernail. Let's just hope they're not the alkies in the gutter in any street in any town or city, although they're pretty damn likely to be, according to the stats.

Talk to them alkies in the gutter. Ask them if they can remember what the recruiting adverts told 'em. Or why they're not off laying bricks.

I don't think of them a lot, don't get me wrong. I don't think of them at all if I can help it – who does, they're only failed fucking soldiers, ain't they? But I always try to give 'em something, if I can. Most of 'em did their best, in a funny kind of way. Didn't they?

I think of poor old Goughie quite a lot though, poor creepy, stupid Johnnie Gough. He worked up into a proper soldier, like the OC had said he would, and he went to fight "Old England's Foe." He was in some vehicle, maybe a Jackal, I don't know what sort for certain, and it found an IED. One killed inside, and Johnnie Gough blown out across the sand on fire, like a Catherine wheel off its pin. He was invalided back, and farmed out to the NHS, and waiting lists, once the army medics had done the little bits the government would pay for.

What was it old Ken had sung?

> *"You haven't an arm and you haven't a leg,*
> *Haroo, haroo.*
> *You haven't an arm and you haven't a leg,*
> *Haroo.*
> *You haven't an arm and you haven't a leg,*
> *You're an eyeless, noseless, chickenless egg.*
> *You'll have to sit out with a bowl and beg –*

237

Johnnie I hardly knew ya."

An eyeless, noseless, chickenless egg. Yeah. That was Goughie. Nice.

And when I see the hearses drive through Wootton Bassett on the telly, and the faces of the guys in uniform, smart and brave and wonderful in their obit photographs, I fucking cry. Not for the gutless bastards who sent them out there, though. Not the lying, stupid, politicians.

Not for them, at all.